Mystery in Spring

Eleanor Watkins

Sarah Grace
Publishing
Dyslexic Friendly

First published 2025 by Sarah Grace Publishing
an imprint of Malcolm Down Publishing ltd.
www.sarahgracepublishing.co.uk

First published 2025 by Grace and Down Publishing
an imprint of Malcolm Down Publishing Ltd.
www.malcolmdown.co.uk

28 27 26 25   7 6 5 4 3 2 1

British Library Cataloguing in Publication Data
A catalogue record for this book is available from the British Library.

ISBN 978-1-917455-04-6

Cover design by Esther Kotecha
Art direction by Sarah Grace

Printed in the UK

Typeface: The Grace Typeface® by 2K Denmark

Contents

CHAPTER

One

Amy, present day

It was raining when they arrived at the cottage – a grey, gentle drizzle that didn't soak you through when you went out in it, but did obscure the view. Amy felt her heart sink. She hadn't wanted to come in the first place, but had hoped at least for some spectacular views she could put on Instagram to impress the others in her class. Not that they'd be very impressed; most of them would be going on overseas trips to exotic places like Thailand or the Maldives or Mexico. A couple of weeks in Wales seemed a pathetic choice by comparison.

'Fferm Fach' read a sign on the gatepost.

'That means "Little Farm",' said Dad, who had been studying Welsh place names. The cottage itself looked grey and lumpish and plain, built on the side of a mountain with its back to the slope, and small windows at the front looking out towards the valley whenever it was visible. With solid stone walls and a slate roof, a chimney at either end and a front door with a porch, it was like a child's drawing of a house; there was a small paved area and flowerbeds with daffodils poking up in front. Boring, really.

Emily was scrambling out of the car. Mum and Dad were out already, opening the boot and taking out their luggage.

'Wake up, Amy,' said Dad in his most hearty, annoying voice. 'We're here! Come and help carry in the stuff.'

Mum was searching for the key, having consulted the printout directions from the owners. 'Got it!' she exclaimed, holding it up triumphantly. 'I hope the water supply's been switched on as they promised. I'm dying for a cup of tea!'

Amy unfolded her long legs and climbed out. She hadn't actually been asleep, but she had been dozing on and off. She hadn't really paid much attention when they'd left the busy main road and begun their climb into the mountains. Now, the silence seemed to cut them off from the rest of the world, along with the misty rain.

'Isn't it amazing?' said Emily, shouldering her purple backpack. 'We could be the only people in the world!'

Amy shuddered. 'What a dreadful idea!'

The front door was solid-looking, ancient oak by the look of it, with metal hinges that creaked a little when it was opened. A few tired-looking pot plants were in the porch. Amy saw her mum look speculatively at them and guessed she'd be watering them ASAP.

Mum opened the door to the right and said, 'Ah, this is the living room, thought so.' She led the way inside, Dad bringing up the rear with most of the luggage. It had a stone-flagged floor, softened with woven rugs, soft cream plastered walls and a wood-burning stove in a wide fireplace, with logs and kindling to hand. It had been lit, casting a gentle warmth to the room; a worn leather sofa and armchairs were arranged around the fireplace. There was also a bookcase with the usual holiday cottage assortment of paperbacks.

'No TV,' said Emily.

'No, we knew there wouldn't be,' said Mum. 'We did tell you! The signal is very dodgy here, it seems. Same for phones. You have to move around and find the best place for reception, maybe even go outside and climb the hill to get a good one. We knew that – it's part of the reason we picked this place, to get away from all that. Wasn't it?' she said, appealing to Dad.

He nodded, dumping down the bags. 'It was.'

'Let's see the rest,' said Emily.

The door across the hall to the left revealed a dining room, slightly smaller than the first room, but with the same stone-flagged floor, beams, window and sturdy furniture. There was a high-backed settle near the fireplace, which was laid with kindling but not lit, and a Welsh dresser with blue and white plates set against one wall. Rustic-looking items hung on the walls – a copper warming pan and a wreath of dried flowers and grasses. A rattan rug was on the floor. Mum opened a door at the back of the room and Amy thought she breathed a sigh of relief. Here was where the conversion work had been done, resulting in a modern kitchen with fitted wood units, breakfast bar, cooker, sink, fridge, kettle, toaster, microwave – everything you'd expect in a holiday cottage.

A bright holiday brochure lay on a counter top, with details of the cottage and some of its history and origins.

Emily picked it up. 'It says that this was originally a farmhouse, not a cottage. The two front rooms and upstairs have been virtually untouched, structurally, except for the fireplaces. These back rooms have been completely remodelled – this would have been the "back kitchen" with a stone sink, copper, and buckets by the sink for pigswill.' She stepped across the tiny lobby to another door. 'This would have been the dairy. Oh!' She broke off, surprised. 'It's the bathroom! It's quite impressive, actually. Look, Ames, even a power shower!'

The bathroom was quite large and long, with floor and walls tiled in the same pale terracotta. It seemed to have everything, from hairdryer to a full-length mirror, a long counter top with another mirror behind it running the whole length, to adjustable stools for doing hair and make-up.

'This place is growing on me,' said Emily, twirling a stool. 'Rustic, but with every comfort as well. I might enjoy this – I think!'

Mum and Dad were discussing water supplies and drainage and septic tanks and other boring things. Amy wandered to the bathroom window. The end of a grey stone building showed through the misty drizzle.

'Those must have been the old farm buildings,' she said.

Emily was consulting the brochure again. 'Yes, there are several of them. Some are tumbling down a bit. It says the plan is to build them all up into holiday places, over time. Like a little holiday village.'

Amy found that she didn't like the idea of a holiday village at all, all slick and organised and probably with a playground and shop and all kinds of amenities. She wasn't too keen on the cottage, but it seemed to be better than a commercial enterprise, even if it was a bit rustic. The modern kitchen and bathroom helped, of course.

Upstairs, accessed by a twisty narrow oak staircase, were three bedrooms. Mum and Dad would have the one at the end, they said. The middle room, across a tiny landing, was actually the largest, with twin beds. Beyond that was another smaller room with a single bed.

'You two can arrange yourselves as you like,' said Mum. 'Share the big room or one can sleep in the small room if you prefer. I know you like your own space. I'll leave you to it. I'm going down to see if we can rustle up something to eat.'

Amy and Emily each had their own rooms at home. They looked at each other, peeked into the small bedroom and looked at each other again.

Emily sighed. 'I think we'll have to share,' she said. 'That little room is so poky. Unless you want it.'

Amy shrugged. It didn't matter much. It was only for a fortnight anyway.

'OK, then,' said Emily. 'Might be a good idea to share. We can dump all our stuff in the little room. It can be a kind of dressing room.'

It was only later, when bags were unpacked, the pie and tomatoes Mum had bought on the way eaten, and everyone was in bed, that Amy wished she had chosen the little room. As soon as she closed her eyes, the thought of Suzy came, as it always did, flooding her with misery and bringing stinging tears to her eyes and sobs to her throat. She wasn't sure whether Emily was asleep in the other bed or not. In case she wasn't and would ask questions, she buried her face in the pillow and pulled the duvet up over her face to muffle the sobs.

CHAPTER

Two

Amy was woken the next morning by her sister's voice yelling, close at hand, 'Hey, Ames! Wake up! Come and look at this.'

Emily had pulled back the curtains and was standing at the window in her pyjamas. Amy groaned and rolled over, but Emily was insistent. 'Ames, you've got to come and see this.' Amy tumbled out of bed and padded barefoot across to the window. She could see at once what all the fuss was about. The rain and mist had cleared, leaving a sparkling spring morning. Their window looked out over the valley, a breathtaking vista of hillside, fields, hedges, small patches of woodland, dropping down to the valley bottom, where a river ran through with a small town huddled on its banks. The occasional farmhouse or cottage dotted the slopes, each mostly with its own small shelter of trees, but there was no sign of life except a plume of smoke rising from the chimneys of one or two of them, and the white shapes of sheep in the fields. On the other side of the river, the land rose again to gentle wooded hills and fields, and the same rolling landscape stretched away to hills in the distance.

'Wow!' said Emily. 'Just wow! Let's go and look at the view from the back.'

They pulled on hoodies and thrust their feet into trainers. Outside, there was a nip in the air despite the blue skies, and a slight touch of white frost was burning off in the sunshine. From the back of the cottage, the view was even more spectacular. The slope was steeper here, rising in a tangle of gorse and whinberry bushes to a high mountain ridge with its head almost in the clouds. Little paths wound up its slopes where generations of sheep had trod, and their descendants roamed freely on the close-cropped turf.

'There are ponies too,' said Emily, pointing to a group of larger animals some distance away. 'And some of the sheep have lambs! Of course, it's lambing time. I wonder if the owners might need help with the lambing?'

Amy pulled a face. Emily wanted to be a vet and would love nothing more than to assist in some messy birthing process. It wasn't her idea of fun at all. 'They look like wild sheep to me,' she said.

'No such thing as wild sheep,' said Emily. 'They all belong to someone. I'm going to get Dad to ask around.'

They were joined by Dad himself coming out of the back door, bringing a whiff from inside of something cooking.

'Mum reckons we have enough supplies for scrambled eggs, toast and tea this morning, but then we'll have to shop for supplies. What a glorious day! Looks better this morning, doesn't it?'

They had to agree it did. 'Where will we shop?' asked Amy.

They had wandered back round to the front of the house, noticing the huddle of grey stone buildings now visible across the yard, which showed this had been a farm. Dad pointed to the cluster of houses on the riverbank far below. 'Down there. That's Hay-on-Wye, the Book Town; that's partly why we came here. Arguably the most famous book centre in the world. A month or so from now, it'll be bursting at the seams hosting one of the world's major literature festivals.'

'It looks like a tiny place,' said Amy, wondering where on earth the big supermarkets could be.

'Oh, it is. But it's amazing. It used to be just another quiet little rural border town. Now people flock here in their tens of thousands, all year round. There are more than thirty bookshops alone, and—' He was well into teacher mode now and had obviously been reading up on local history. Amy sighed. Now he'd probably go on for half the morning. Her hands were getting chilly and she pulled her hoodie sleeves down over them. It was a relief when Mum called from the kitchen, 'Breakfast's ready, guys!'

They ate at the breakfast bar in the kitchen, showered in the chic bathroom and got dressed.

Mum took the chance while she and Amy were clearing the breakfast things to ask, 'Are you OK, Amy?' She often asked this in the mornings; Amy knew from her mirror that she sometimes started the day looking pale, with dark shadows under her eyes. She had also heard Mum and Dad discussing her when they thought she couldn't hear, and knew they worried about her. She let her hair swing forwards to hide her face, and turned away to hang up the tea towel.

'I'm fine, Mum.'

Her mother patted her arm. 'That's good, sweetheart. We're hoping this holiday will really help.'

Amy sighed. They meant well, but nothing could help, really. And they didn't know the half of it, she thought sadly.

The road into Hay was all downhill, narrow and twisty with some very steep places that Dad said must be treacherous in winter. A faint haze of green was beginning to cloak the hedgerows, and there were primroses starring the steep grass banks. There was only room for single vehicles; there were passing places at intervals. No one seemed to be about, and they arrived in Hay without having to back up once.

The big main car park was filling up fast. 'Easter holidaymakers, like us,' said Dad. 'Only to be expected, I suppose.'

They decided they'd park and have a quick look round before going to the Co-op on the outskirts of town to stock up on supplies. 'We'll need to get frozen stuff, so we'll have to go straight home with it,' said Mum.

The town was dominated by the castle, a magnificent grey granite structure, recently restored, parts of it dating back to the Norman occupation of Britain. They could see people high up on a viewing platform, and others sitting drinking coffee on an outdoor terrace.

'We'll do a proper tour one of these days,' promised Dad.

Around the castle, twisty little streets wound their way downwards towards the river; a clock tower stood proudly chiming every fifteen minutes, and people sat at outdoor tables at several bistro-type cafés. Antique shops and boutiques rubbed shoulders with more mundane greengrocers and grocery stores. And of course, the bookshops. Small bookshops, and large. Bookshops with intriguing names like Murder and Mayhem, Green Ink Booksellers, The Old Electric Shop and so on. A huge warehouse bookshop with a dim, inviting interior, an enormous one that had once been a cinema, an honesty bookshop in the castle grounds where you took what you wanted and paid what you could afford. Amy could see Dad's eyes light up, and Mum's too. Both teachers, they each had aspirations of writing books themselves, Dad a historical novel he'd been mulling over for a while, Mum, the more practical one, a cookery book of country recipes. Amy knew they'd both love nothing more than to plunge into one of the bookshops and immerse themselves in the atmosphere. She groaned inwardly. Then the groan turned into an audible gasp. A group of girls her age had sauntered past, managing to consult their phones and chatter and giggle at the same time. Amy felt her heart beginning to race. For a moment she'd been convinced that one of them, a tall blonde in a white hoodie, black leggings and silver trainers, had been Suzy. She even walked and tossed her ponytail as Suzy had done.

It wasn't her, of course. Suzy would never walk down a street again. Mum was peering at her. 'Are you all right, Amy? You've gone quite pale.'

Blow Mum and her sharp eyes! Amy hoped she hadn't noticed the likeness. The girls had disappeared round a corner. They were passing a place called Shepherd's that seemed to be an ice-cream parlour. She said, 'Can we get ice creams?'

The ice creams were made from sheep's milk and were delicious. They ate them sitting on a raised stone patio area opposite the parlour, which seemed to be a popular gathering place. 'The old butter and cheese markets are just behind us,' said Dad, consulting his guide. It was pleasant sitting in the sun, watching the world go by, but Mum reminded them they were on a mission.

'We'll come back other days,' she promised. 'Explore properly and go to the castle. Maybe market day would be good. We'd better get the shopping done, then I can stop worrying about food.'

'Mustn't forget we'll be going to another country for that,' said Dad solemnly. Both girls stared at him. 'What do you mean?'

'We're right on the border here,' said Dad. 'Part of Hay is actually in England. The Co-op is just over the border. Offa's Dyke is actually the boundary, but just here it's the Dulas Brook. We'll be going over the bridge—'

He was off again in lecturing mode. Amy and Emily looked at each other. The sooner he started his writing, the better, and then perhaps he'd forget about being a teacher for a while.

CHAPTER

Three

'I think we'll go to church this morning,' announced Dad over the cornflakes on Sunday morning. Both girls groaned. They had spent the previous day hiking in the hills, and had climbed to the very top of Lord Hereford's Knob or, in Welsh, the Twmpa. It had been a good day for a hike, dry and clear, but with a breeze cool enough to refresh toiling bodies with packs on their backs. Heather, bracken and whinberries were sprouting fresh growth, and sheep grazed on spring grass. They had reached the summit triumphant, and Emily had raised her arms to the skies and shouted, 'We did it! We're on top of the world!'

Amy had gazed at the panorama spread below in all directions, the fields and hills and tiny dwellings, sheep and cattle on the lower slopes, a tiny toy tractor working in a field far below. It had made her feel very small, but at the same time strangely part of it all, with a kind of joy that surprised her. Mum was busy passing out drinks and unpacking their picnic lunch. Dad, being Dad, had first pointed out the half-hidden roof of their own cottage, Fferm Fach, with its back to them, and then embarked on a history lesson for their edification.

'The mountain opposite is Hay Bluff. Most climbers go for that first. At its base is a popular spot for people to stop and park their cars. There are some large granite formations there; the locals call them the 'Standing Stones'. There are several hollows around there which are old bomb craters; there's a theory that bombers were on their way to Birmingham but jettisoned their bombs in the mountains.' He'd pointed to the road below them, clinging to the base of Hay Bluff and wending its way between the two peaks, disappearing round a bend among more grassy hills. 'That's called the Gospel Pass. There are various theories about why it has that name. I must look into that a bit more.'

Maybe it was the name of the Gospel Pass which had given him the idea of going to church. They were all quite stiff from the unaccustomed climbing the day before, and Amy had looked forward to a quiet morning lazing around.

Mum looked surprised. 'We don't usually go. Do you mean the church in Hay – St Mary's, I think it is?'

Dad shook his head. 'No, I've been reading up, and there's an old chapel not far away from here as the crow flies, on the hillside, and there's a lot of history attached to it. I don't think there are services every week now, but I looked it up and there's one today.'

They were all quite relieved that it would be in the afternoon. They could at least have a quiet morning just chilling. Dad mentioned that a bit of revision might not come amiss; they'd brought books with them and had to remember that Emily's GCSEs were coming up, and that Amy would have to seriously think about her options. They sighed and rolled their eyes, but at least it gave them the opportunity to go to their bedroom, lie down and check the signals on their phones.

'Do you suppose we'll have to dress up for church?' asked Amy when they were upstairs. 'I've only got jeans and leggings, nothing fancy.'

'Then jeans and leggings it'll be,' said Emily. 'If they don't like it, tough!' She rolled over on her stomach and looked across at Amy. 'By the way, Ames, there's something I wanted to say, without the 'rents about. Do you know you talk in your sleep? And sometimes seem to be having nightmares?'

Amy knew about the nightmares, of course, which were almost always about Suzy. She didn't know she talked in her sleep, and didn't dare ask what she said. Her sister seemed not to have missed a thing, because she added, 'And you cry in your sleep too.' She propped her chin on her hands and her brown eyes were concerned. Amy froze. It was a good thing that Emily thought she was asleep when she cried in the night, and Amy wasn't going to enlighten her. She put her hand over her eyes. Sharing a room was worse than she'd imagined. Unlike some sisters she knew, she and Em usually got on well together, apart from the odd scrap or argument about borrowed clothes or belongings, and she didn't want to offend her sister by being the one to suggest she slept in the other room. In the event, she didn't have to, because Emily said hesitantly, 'I was just wondering if we'd be better off in separate rooms, like at home. I could go in the little room, if you like.'

Amy felt a stab of relief. 'No need,' she said quickly. 'I'll go in there. I know I have nightmares . . . didn't realise I talked as well. Sorry. Is that OK?'

Emily sounded relieved too. 'OK with me. I worry a bit about you, though, Ames. D'you think you ought to see a counsellor or someone, about Suzy and all that?'

'No, I'm fine,' said Amy quickly. 'Don't worry about me. Probably my age, as Grandma would say.' She gave a slightly forced laugh. 'Don't say anything to Mum and Dad, they'll only fuss. We'll just say we decided to have separate rooms, OK? We can move our stuff this evening.'

'Right,' said Emily. She might have said more, but her phone flashed to say she had a text, and she rolled over to answer it. Amy breathed a sigh of relief. A sticky moment seemed to have passed.

The chapel seemed a rather lonely place, Amy thought, set down in the middle of fields in the lee of the Twmpa, a small, simple, rather Gothic-looking building with a smaller building to the side. It was reached by a gate leading into the large grassy graveyard surrounding the chapel. A hawthorn tree stood near the gate. The inside was simple with plastered walls, and a pulpit to one side at the front looking out over rows of solid oak pews. They need not have worried about dressing up for church. There were several older ladies in the congregation who seemed to be in their Sunday best; one or two even wore hats. But most of the others were quite casually dressed, and the girls didn't feel out of place in their jeans and hoodies. The pews proved to be rather hard, straight-backed and uncomfortable, despite efforts that had been made to soften them with long cushions. 'So that you don't fall asleep during the sermon,' whispered Dad. They were welcomed from the front as visitors, so that people turned their heads to look. The singing was surprisingly tuneful with a good rhythm, thought Amy, although the words were unfamiliar.

The speaker seemed to be visiting for the day. He greeted them in both English and Welsh, and he had a Welsh-sounding name too. Amy wondered if he would speak in Welsh right through the service. He didn't; he spoke English, though with a very marked Welsh accent.

In spite of the cushions, the pews got more and more uncomfortable. Amy fidgeted until she discovered another chunky cushion on the floor. 'A hassock,' whispered Dad. 'To put your feet on. Or kneel on.'

The hassock was firm and helped a lot. In spite of the improvement, she felt her mind wandering. She glanced sideways at Emily, wondering again what she had talked about in her sleep. But when the speaker began to mention God, she felt herself tense up inside, and tried hard to let her mind wander again. She had attempted to pray to God about Suzy, had pleaded and wept and lit candles and made promises. It hadn't worked. God didn't answer. Or, he didn't care. Or it was her fault? She hadn't prayed right? Or was there just no God at all, despite all these people in this place who obviously believed in him? Whatever the reason, she was done with him.

The sermon was drawing to a close. She suddenly became aware again, as the speaker finished with, 'Whatever else you take away this afternoon, remember this. God knows you by your name, and all about you. And he loves you.'

Amy was startled. Was he a mind-reader or something? Then everyone was getting to their feet again to sing the final hymn.

She wanted to get away as quickly as possible and get back to the cottage. But it had been announced that tea would follow in the stone building opposite and everyone was welcome. Dad and Mum thought they should stay and get to know the local people a little.

The girls were surprised when a youngish couple waved and smiled as though they knew them, and their parents waved back. The couple came over and greeted them warmly.

'These are our daughters, Emily and Amy,' said Mum, pushing the girls forwards. 'Girls, this is David and Ceri Powell, from the next farm to Ffern Fach, and the owners of the cottage.' They shook hands and murmured greetings.

The four of them were steered towards the stone building, which was newly renovated. Ceri seemed a very pleasant person, fair-haired and fresh-faced, and soon she and Mum were chattering away like old friends. Her husband, dark and stocky, was quieter, but he and Dad seemed to be hitting it off too. The girls trailed behind. There were some children, but no one their own age. Emily was soon drawn in, though. Dad must have mentioned her interest in animals, because he beckoned her over, and Amy saw her sister's face grow pink and animated as they talked.

Someone pressed a plate with a yellow napkin into her hand. 'Just help yourself, bach,' she was told. 'From London, are you?'

It seemed to be a place where everyone liked to know everyone else's business. She murmured a reply, and began to pile her plate from the lavish selection of sandwiches, sausage rolls, cakes and tarts of all kinds, set out on a long table. *This would be Suzy's idea of a nightmare*, she thought, and almost smiled until she remembered. Suddenly, the chattering people, the cheerful faces, the enquiring looks that came her way were all too much. She edged her way through the bodies eager for tea and food, and made her way out through the open door and into the green and quiet of the graveyard.

CHAPTER

Four

The chatter of the tearoom faded away as Amy wandered around the grassy enclosure surrounding the chapel. Beyond, fields spread out without a dwelling in sight; below, the ground gently fell away to the panorama of the valley. Birds twittered in the branches of hawthorns and hazels in the hedgerow; she could hear the bleating baby cries of young lambs and the answering deeper tones of their grazing mothers.

Munching from the plate in her hand, Amy walked slowly, following the inside of the surrounding wall, which was lined with the headstones of the departed. More gravestones were dotted about among the grass in a seemingly haphazard way, nothing like the neat rows she had seen in a cemetery back home, the cemetery that had become Suzy's final resting place. She swallowed a mouthful of cake and could suddenly eat no more, crumbling the last of the cake onto the grass. It wouldn't matter here; she guessed there'd be plenty of birds and insects that would clean up the crumbs. She swallowed again and began to read the inscriptions on the headstones. Some were surprisingly recent; evidently burials still took place here. Others looked ancient and somewhat neglected, the grass long against them and moss growing over the granite. She read: 'Hannah Jane Jones, 1835-1895, dearly beloved wife of Edwin Ifor Jones and mother of Isaac, Edwina, Martha, Dora and Samuel. Well done, good and faithful servant, enter into thy rest.' Lower down was an inscription to Edwin Ifor Jones, who seemed to have outlived his wife by several years, and another grave nearby that stated 'Martha Olwen Jones, aged 10 years. Safe in the arms of Jesus.' Whatever happened to her, wondered Amy, and found that there were tears in her eyes, especially when she saw an even smaller and newer gravestone that stated simply: 'Katherine Jane Pritchard, 2008-2013. At peace.' *Not long ago at all*, she thought, and felt a tear trickle down her cheek. She pulled herself together, and decided she'd better stop this and go to find the others.

Emily was bubbling over by the time Amy rejoined the rest of the family and they were making their way to the car. 'Wondered where you'd gone. Guess what! David Parry says they're very busy with the lambing at the moment and they could do with someone else to help. I can go there whenever I want to – it's only a couple of fields away!'

Amy opened the car door. 'Oh, great! I'm going to be left on my own, then.'

'Don't be like that. Actually, they've asked us both over for tea and Welsh cakes, and to have a look round. It'll be fun!'

Emily refused to let her bubble be burst. She chattered on all the way home, and didn't stop as they were getting out of the car and going into the cottage.

'David had a look at my hands, and he says they're just what's needed, small but strong and with long fingers.' She waggled her fingers in the air. 'Sometimes, lambs get stuck in the birth canal, or the wrong part is coming first, and they have to be put right before they can be born. Or they're extra big. It needs someone with small hands to go in and feel about and put them right. Just imagine, I might even actually get to deliver a lamb myself!' She clasped her small, strong, long-fingered hands together in ecstasy.

'Oh, don't!' begged Amy. 'I've just had a big tea and you're making me queasy!'

Dad said it was good to see Emily so enthusiastic, and Mum said they must be sure to get Ceri's recipe for Welsh cakes. Amy said no more. She didn't want to be a killjoy, but she didn't want to hear any more gory details, either.

Emily had thankfully gone off on a slightly new tack by the time they were rearranging their bedrooms. She gathered up an armful of her clothes from the smaller room and dumped them on Amy's vacated bed in the large one.

'David has lots of farming books and vet books too because, guess what? He trained to be a vet himself. Then he gave it up to take on the family farm when his dad died. The training must be well useful, though! He says he'll lend me the books, and explain bits I don't understand. Did you know sheep can get all kinds of illnesses, like liver fluke and pulpy kidney and foot rot? Do you want me to help you make up your bed? Are you sure you'll be OK in this room?'

'I'll be fine,' said Amy, looking around the small room. She couldn't help adding, 'It'll be a relief not to hear you going on about sheep diseases with disgusting names!'

They found the bed linen and duvet and made up the bed together. Besides the bed, there was only room for a slim wardrobe and a bedside table with a lamp on it. Emily looked round. 'It's very poky. Are you sure you don't mind sleeping here?'

'As I've said twenty million times, no, I don't mind!' said Amy. She looked around at the room. It had a very faded, old-fashioned kind of wallpaper with roses on it. She quite liked it, though Emily didn't.

'This must be the bedroom Ceri said they're going to renovate next, when they can afford it. It might be quite pretty with a subtle shade of paint and some wall mirrors, with fairy lights and some nice cushions. This paper must have been here for decades. I bet there are layers of other wallpapers underneath this one.' She picked at a loose corner of wallpaper behind the flowery curtains, which also had roses on them, though a different kind to the wallpaper. 'Yes, thought so – look, at least four layers before you get to the plaster.' She gave a little tug, and then said, 'Oh, sugar! It's so old a whole flap has come loose. Good thing it's going to be redecorated. And if I pull the curtain across a bit more, it won't show.' She leaned closer. 'Ames, come and look. There's something written on the plaster underneath. It's a name. Come and see! Sarah something.'

They both peered at the small patch of exposed whitish plaster. Sure enough, there was some spidery brown handwriting. 'Sarah Rees,' read Amy. 'B July 22nd 1908. BA April 19th 1922.' They looked at each other.

'What does it mean? The B could mean she was born on that date. But what does the BA mean?' said Emily.

'Isn't BA Bachelor of Arts?' said Amy. 'A university degree? But she was too young for that.'

'I don't think girls would have gone to uni in those days,' said Emily. 'Not farm girls, anyway. And she was only fourteen, your age. Unless she was a child prodigy or something.' They both giggled. 'Maybe the Parrys would know something about it. Their family seems to have been about here a long time. We could ask tomorrow.' She yawned. 'I'm tired now. I'm going to bed. Are you sure you'll be OK here?'

'Yes,' said Amy. 'Yes, yes, yes!' She picked up a pillow from the freshly made bed and brandished it, and Emily made for the door.

'OK, OK. Goodnight, then.'

Later, when Amy was in bed in the little room, she found her thoughts returning to Sarah Rees, the girl who had slept here 100 years ago and may have been a genius. She was still thinking about her as she drifted off. For once, she didn't sob herself to sleep. She didn't have nightmares either, or none that she remembered. She didn't know whether she'd talked in her sleep, but there was no one to hear. She liked the little room, and in the morning realised she'd had the best sleep for weeks, and seemed to have a feeling she'd almost forgotten – a sense of peace.

CHAPTER

Five

A few days later, the opportunity came for visiting the Parrys at their farm. The previous day had been spent exploring the town, and in particular, Hay Castle. Everyone agreed that the castle was brilliant and not boring at all. They'd read and watched videos of some of the history of the castle, parts of it dating back to Norman times, and heard the fascinating story of Matilda, wife of William de Breos, who had lived there. Legend had it that she was a giantess, who had carried stones from the river in her apron for the building of the castle, which she had achieved in a single night. A piece of stone, measuring 1ft by 9ft, had lodged in her shoe; she had taken it out and flung it clean across the river, all the way to the village of Llowes, three miles away, where it could be seen at the parish church there to this day, a huge chunk of granite, known as the 'Moll Walbee' stone.

'We must go and check that out while we're here,' said Dad. They had climbed the steep steps to the dizzying heights of the viewing platform, with the roofs of the town spread out like an aerial photograph, and descended more steps to the dim and chilly dungeon. They had studied the more recent history of Richard Booth, an eccentric Oxford graduate, who became the self-appointed King of Hay in the 1970s, had opened his first bookshop there almost sixty years ago, and so began a bookselling reputation that had spread worldwide. And they had enjoyed a refreshing coffee in the restaurant, and later, found a cosy little café back at ground level to have lunch. So inspired had Dad been by the history of the place that he wanted to spend the next day writing notes and checking details online for his planned future novel. Mum was quite content to stay near the cottage and read some of the books she had bought in the town. And Emily was itching to go to the Parry farm to see the animals and learn more about them, so the day seemed planned. Amy was quite happy with the arrangement. They phoned Ceri, who said she was making Welsh cakes that very morning and it would be a good time.

'You can't really get lost on the way,' said Dad. 'Their farm can't be seen from here, but if you go through that gate at the end of our lane and walk across two fields, you'll dip down into the valley where it is.'

And so it was. They walked through a field with just grass in it, and then another with some brown and white cattle, and there was the Parry farm below, tucked away in its sheltering hollow, a group of mellow stone buildings within a cluster of sheltering trees. Amy was wary of the cattle, which seemed to have gathered in a bunch and were all staring curiously at them. 'I hope there aren't any bulls there,' she said nervously.

Emily was briskly reassuring. 'No, there aren't. It's not the bulls you have to worry about anyway, usually. It's the cows with young calves. They're very protective. But these are all young cattle, heifers and bullocks. They're very nosy and they might follow us. But they won't harm us.'

Amy was impressed with the knowledge of farm animals that her sister had already gained. Just the same, she breathed a sigh of relief when they were through the gate into the farmyard and the young cattle were safely on the other side.

The Parry farm was a much bigger affair than the one at Fferm Fach. Old stone buildings and modern corrugated iron and concrete ones rubbed shoulders around a large, concreted farmyard. Amy had half-expected chickens to be scratching about, or ducks quacking, but the yard was clean and bare, except for a very large green tractor parked near one of the buildings. More machines could be seen inside. At the far end of the yard stood the grey stone farmhouse, large and solid and looking as though it had stood there for centuries, although Amy noticed that a row of solar panels had been added to the grey slate roof. A tabby cat lay asleep on a low wall surrounding a paved front garden, bordered by a mass of golden daffodils.

'It's very quiet, isn't it?' said Emily as they made their way across the yard.

She spoke too soon. Suddenly a chorus of loud warning barking came from somewhere out of sight, and two large black and white dogs came from behind the house and descended upon them. Amy's heart pounded; she wondered if they should run, or climb the gate. But Emily was equal to the situation. 'They're OK, look at their tails,' she said. The two black and white tails were waving in a friendly way, and the dogs stopped barking as they reached the girls, and sat down, tongues lolling in a couple of doggy grins.

David Parry appeared round the house and called 'Fly! Patch! Quiet, now! They're OK, girls, just greeting you. Come on in, I was just having my morning coffee.'

He ushered them round to the back of the house and through a weatherbeaten back door, passed a pile of Wellington boots and coats in a back porch into a stone-flagged farmhouse kitchen with a large, scrubbed table in the middle and a Rayburn. Ceri, in a striped apron over her jeans and jumper, was turning Welsh cakes on a griddle – round, golden circles that smelled of spices and were dotted with sultanas. A pile of already cooked ones was cooling on a rack.

'Come in, girls,' she greeted them cheerfully. 'Sit down, and David will make you some coffee.'

They pulled out chairs and sat down at the table. David served them coffee in bright mugs with farm scenes, and put a plate of Welsh cakes on the table. He did not sit down again himself. 'Sorry, but I've got to get back to the lambing shed. Come and find me when you're ready – it's the big one at the other end of the yard.'

He left by the back door and they saw him stride across the yard, the two dogs at his heels. The Welsh cakes were as delicious as they looked, but Emily declined a third. She was itching to get out among the sheep. Ceri laughed as she excused herself, pulled on her Wellingtons and followed in David's footsteps.

'She's keen, isn't she, your sister?'

Amy nodded. 'Yes. She can't wait to get into vet school.'

Ceri placed the last of the Welsh cakes on the wire rack and sat down herself. 'And how about you? Do you have plans for the future?'

Amy felt herself tense up inside. She didn't like talking about herself, you never knew what might come out. She shrugged. 'Haven't decided yet.'

Ceri poured herself coffee and stirred it thoughtfully. 'I know we don't know each other very well yet, but I've noticed you have a sad look about you sometimes. We border Welsh are known for being nosy, so tell me to shut up if you like. But is there something that troubles you? Could I help? Believe it or not, I was a trained youth counsellor before I became a farmer's wife.'

Amy began to feel panic rise. If she said that she'd lost a friend, who knew where the conversation might lead? It could all get horribly out of control. Maybe she'd better just go out and find Emily. Then she remembered, with a sense of relief, the writing they had found on the bedroom wall in the cottage. She said, 'I'm OK. But there's something I wanted to ask you about.'

'Ask away.'

'Well, I'm sleeping in the small bedroom at the cottage. And the other day, we accidentally tore a bit of wallpaper by the window, and there was some writing underneath.' She paused. 'I'm really sorry, we didn't mean to tear it. We can stick it back if you like.'

Ceri laughed. 'Please, don't worry! That room's going to be all stripped down anyway. Writing, you say? What kind of writing?'

'A name,' said Amy. 'And dates. The name was Sarah Rees, and the first date was 1908 – there was a B before it so that must have been when she was born, but then underneath, it said BA April 1922. Do you know what it might mean?'

Ceri frowned. 'No idea about the BA bit. And I don't think the family there was called Rees, either. David's grandfather bought the farm from a family called Hughes, I believe, and they'd been there for generations. It's been in this family ever since. I don't know who Sarah Rees could be.'

'Would David know?' asked Amy.

Ceri laughed. 'Well, he might. But he's always too busy to have much of an interest in local history.' She paused. 'There's a lot of old family stuff in boxes in the attic here – photos, and letters and bills, all kinds of things. They must have been brought from Fferm Fach when David's grandfather bought the farm. There might be something there to give you a clue if we looked through them.' She laughed ruefully. 'No time for that at lambing time, I'm afraid. It's go-go-go all day and half the night for a few weeks.'

'I could look through them,' said Amy eagerly, then stopped and felt herself blush. 'I mean, if you didn't mind ...'

Ceri laughed again. 'I don't mind at all, and I don't suppose David would, either, but I'd have to ask him. If you really want to do that. Sorting through dusty old stuff in an attic wouldn't be my idea of holiday fun! You're really keen on finding out about this mysterious Sarah, aren't you?'

Amy nodded, embarrassed. She couldn't quite explain it, but ever since they'd discovered that scribbled name, she'd had Sarah on her mind. Was that writing a message for someone? Was it in some kind of code? And how was it that no one had seen it before, in more than 100 years, not until she, Amy Reynolds, happened to be sleeping in that room?

Ceri was getting to her feet. 'Sorry, Amy, you're welcome to stay as long as you like, or go and join your sister, but I've really got to get on . . . David's dinner to get started, and lots to do.'

Amy wandered out to find Emily, who she discovered had just witnessed the delivery of twin lambs, and with her sleeves rolled up, was helping to rub down one of the bleating, staggering newborns. She was in her element, and even Amy caught a little of her wonder at the new births. Emily was full of her morning's experiences all the way home, and was thrilled that she'd been asked to come back. But even before the cottage came into view, Amy's mind had returned to Sarah Rees. She'd go back soon and ask to see the old letters for possible clues.

That evening, they all went to see a film at the rather posh cinema in Hay, attached to one of the bookshops. The plot was fast-paced and gripping. But as they went to bed, Amy's mind was already drifting away from the drama and back to the mysterious Sarah. Her last thoughts were of her as she slipped into sleep.

CHAPTER

Six

Sarah, early 1920s

'Thump! Thump! Thump!' The sound was muffled but persistent, rising from the bedroom floor and refusing to be ignored. Sarah groaned and turned over in bed. The mattress was hard, the feather bed lumpy, but infinitely more inviting to stay in rather than get out of bed and stand shivering in the chilly spring dawn. Even so, she held her breath for a moment and hoped the sound would stop. But no – thump, thump, thump; there it was again. She sighed and got out of bed, hurrying into her clothes as quickly as possible. A quick dip of a flannel into the cold water in the jug on the washstand, a rub over her face, and a swift brush of her brown hair was all there was time for. She tiptoed out of the room, through the larger one where the children were not stirring yet, down the creaky stairs.

In the front parlour, Granny Hughes regarded her crossly from dark eyes that were still gimlet-sharp. She wore a nightcap and a voluminous flannel nightgown, and was sitting up in bed with her stick raised for another series of taps on the ceiling, conveniently sited immediately below Sarah's little room. Her false teeth reposed in a glass of water beside the bed. She greeted Sarah with: 'Ah, there you are, girl, about time!'

Sarah felt irritation rise, but she forced herself to say pleasantly, 'Good morning, Mrs Hughes. Can I get you something?'

'Aye, you can get me a good hot cup of chamomile tea. My rheumatics have kept me awake all night, and I didn't sleep a wink.'

Sarah doubted that, having noticed audible snores from below when she woke briefly in the night. She hurried through to the kitchen, where a dim glow from behind the bars of the grate showed that there was life there still. A few puffs of the bellows and a handful of morning wood soon coaxed it into a cheerful blaze, and Sarah transferred the big black kettle from the hob to the hook over the fire. While it came to the boil, she began breakfast preparations, and by the time it was singing, movement from above showed that the rest of the household was waking up. When she had made the tea and delivered it to the old lady, the man of the house and head of the family had descended the stairs and was sitting in his chair by the fire to put on his boots. Above, Sarah could hear the wail of the baby and its mother soothing it, and children's voices raised in argument. A new day at Fferm Fach had begun.

Mr Penry Hughes was stocky, dark-haired and taciturn. He grunted a good morning to Sarah's greeting and stumped out of the back door to begin his morning rounds. Sarah looked at the grandfather clock ticking in a corner of the kitchen and sighed. Ten past seven already. The children must be got up, washed, dressed, breakfasted, lunches packed, and sent on their long walk to school. The water for porridge was on to boil, table laid, eggs and milk and butter fetched from the dairy. A shriek and a wail sounded from upstairs. Mrs Hughes junior came down, carrying the baby. She looked weary already.

'Teething again, up half the night with this one. Go and see to the children, Sarah, do!' she said crossly. She dumped the baby into the cradle near the fireplace, where he began to cry fretfully. Sarah had been about to stir porridge into the water but put down the spoon. If breakfast was late, she couldn't help it. She couldn't be in two places at once.

Upstairs, the two small boys were only half-dressed and were rolling on their bed and thumping each other with shrieks of laughter. Ten-year-old Nancy had somehow got into a tangle with her apron strings and was vainly appealing to her twelve-year-old sister for help. But Alice seemed more interested in examining her face in the small hand mirror. Sarah sighed and said, trying to sound authoritative, 'Teddy and Tom, stop that! Nancy, come here and let me sort out that tangle.'

Alice threw her a look which said without words, 'Don't you dare order me about as well! You're just a servant here!' Sarah busied herself untangling Nancy's apron strings.

She was only two years older than Alice, and both of them knew it. Sometimes Alice was friendly, and they'd even shared some confidences with each other, but she was moody too and had a tongue that sometimes seemed as sharp as her grandmother's. She said tragically, 'There's a great big spot on my nose! Can you get me some of that ointment Mother has, Sarah? I can't go to school like this.'

Sarah could barely see the tiny spot that Alice was pointing at. Nobody would ever notice it. She said shortly, 'I don't know where it is. Teddy, come here and put your stockings on!'

Mrs Hughes' voice sounded from below, above the noise of the baby's wails. 'Sarah, come down here and watch the baby and finish the porridge! I must go and do the milking.'

Nice for you, thought Sarah sourly. She herself would far rather escape from the tumult indoors, take the milking buckets and go out to the peace of the cowshed to sit on a stool and tuck her head into the warm flank of a cow, with no sound except the peaceful munching of jaws on hay from the manger, and the swish of milk into the buckets. She even liked the earthy smell of warm cow and hay and manure. She had done the milking before, at the time Mrs Hughes had given birth to William, and for a while afterwards, and become skilful and swift at the job, and had enjoyed it. She suspected Mrs Hughes enjoyed it too, and enjoyed even more the respite from the hustle and bustle of the mornings.

By the time Mrs Hughes returned, with two buckets of foaming fresh milk, the baby had been pacified, the children fed, lunches packed, and they were heading off on the three-mile walk across fields and open mountain to the school in the village. Mr Hughes had done his morning rounds and was sitting down to his own breakfast. Sarah was looking forward to her porridge too, but first there was Granny Hughes to be served with hers, and she had to fulfil any other tasks she might require.

'Another two lambs this morning,' said Mr Hughes, after he had bowed his head and proclaimed grace over the table. 'Soon be coming thick and fast.'

'And then it'll be up all hours with them, never mind this one,' said his wife, indicating William who was now sitting up in his high chair chewing on a crust that Sarah had smeared with some honey.

Mr Hughes grunted. He was a man of few words. His wife more than made up for this, and grumbled a great deal. Sarah had noticed that the grumbles were increasingly directed towards herself, finding fault and apportioning blame for things that were not always Sarah's responsibility. It wasn't fair and she resented it, but it wasn't going to last forever. She'd only agreed to come for two years, and only because her mother needed the money she took home on her days off. In less than two years, her brother Walter would be leaving school and taking a job, and here at Fferm Fach, Alice would leave school too, and would stay home to help her mother. Sarah just had to stick it out. Stirring her tea, she went off into a pleasant daydream of what she might do when she was free. Would she train to be a school teacher? Might she get another job as a shop assistant, or a clerk, or even a secretary? She had done well at school, and was sure she could learn quickly. Might she even earn so much money that her mother would want for nothing for the rest of her life?

Mrs Hughes' voice cut in. 'Look sharp, Sarah! There's the dairy work to do and the henhouse to clean out. And don't forget it's our day for doing upstairs. No time to sit about!'

To be fair, Eira Hughes didn't sit about herself, except when feeding the baby. Nobody sat about for long at

Fferm Fach. Penry Hughes had pushed back his chair and departed to the outdoors. Sarah sighed, gulped down the rest of her tea and began to clear the table. It looked like another busy day.

CHAPTER

Seven

Saturday was even busier. There was no morning rush of sending children off to school, but everything else went on in the same way – cows to be fed, milked and turned out, hens, ducks, hissing geese and a pig to feed, dairy work to be done, not to mention housework and the needs of the family to attend to. It was not quite lambing time; lambs were born later here than in the more temperate lowlands, but the pregnant ewes had to be inspected several times a day.

Despite being the wife of a hard-working hill farmer and the mother of a large family, Eira Hughes was also very houseproud, having worked for a while in her younger days at a manor house. Therefore, certain standards had to be maintained and a routine adhered to; washing on a Monday, ironing on Tuesday, baking on Wednesday. Saturday was housework day, with extra cleaning, which meant scrubbing the stone-flagged floors of the kitchen and back kitchen, something of a thankless task when several pairs of boots constantly brought in mud and manure from the farmyard. It meant washing down the stone salting slabs in the dairy and scrubbing the floor there too. Then there were the many items of bric-a-brac in the front parlour to be dusted, to the accompaniment of scolding and fault-finding from old Mrs Hughes, if that lady was having a bad day. If there was time, it meant turning out a cupboard or two and tidying the shelves. The two girls were expected to take their share of the work, and the little boys had their allotted tasks too, but more often than not succeeded in getting underfoot and causing extra work.

Today, though, it seemed that Alice and Nancy were the ones getting into the most trouble. Set to stripping beds and changing sheets, they had decided to have fun by playing games, twisting the sheets into long ropes and dangling them from the bedroom window, daring each other to climb down and be escaping prisoners, accompanied by much giggling. Their mother was furious. 'What a waste of time! And look at those sheets, there's a rip in one corner. Alice, you're almost grown up, what are you thinking?'

Alice ventured to defend herself. 'It was just a bit of fun! And the sheets are to be washed anyway.' Nancy looked scared, half-hiding behind her sister.

Eira seemed ready to explode. 'Don't dare to answer me back, miss! Get those beds changed, and then I'll find you plenty else to do. I was going to send you off to Y Dyffryn this afternoon with a clutch of duck eggs for Beth Parry, but now I'm thinking you can stop at home and clean the brasses instead.'

Alice's face fell. 'Aw, Mam! I was looking forward to going to Y Dyffryn! I'm sorry for messing about. I never meant any harm. Please!'

Nancy looked as though she might cry, standing there twisting a corner of the sheet, but their mother was not about to relent.

'No, you both need to learn a lesson. Sarah shall go instead.'

Alice threw Sarah a look of pure resentment, but she knew better than to say any more. So it was, that after dinner, the two girls were to be found sulkily sitting at the kitchen table with an array of brass candlesticks, horse brasses and bric-a-brac spread out around them on old newspapers, together with a box of brass powder and a pile of polishing rags. Sarah left them to it and set out across the fields with a basket on her arm. The basket contained twelve pale-green duck's eggs nestled on a bed of hay. There was a belief that hens made better mothers than ducks, and Eira had long promised eggs to her young neighbour when she had a broody hen. Sarah felt her spirits rise. It was so good to be out in the fresh air, with a brisk breeze cool on her face and the first tender green of new grass under her feet. She dawdled a little when she was out of sight of Ffrem Fach, making the outing last as long as possible. The Parry farm lay quiet in its hollow, a plume of smoke rising from its chimney. And there was Beth Parry, crossing the yard after feeding her chickens. Her round face broke into a smile as she heard the creak of the yard gate. 'Good afternoon, Sarah! How are you, bach? And I do believe you've brought the duck eggs that Mrs Hughes promised me. Let's take them straight to old Biddy – she'll be pleased!'

They found the broody hen clucking fussily in her coop, fluffing out her feathers and rearranging her nest. While Beth lifted her off, protesting, and offered her corn, Sarah slipped the eggs into the warm nest. The brown hen resented the disturbance but was delighted to find eggs when she was allowed to return, tucking them away carefully beneath her. Sarah and Beth smiled. 'It'll be a job to shift her now for the next three weeks,' said Beth. 'And she won't care that they're ducklings not chicks – well, not until they find some water and want to swim, that'll puzzle her a bit!'

They both laughed. Sarah liked Beth, what she had seen of her, only eight years or so older then herself, pretty and plump and lively.

'Now, will you come in for a cup of tea and a piece of bara brith,[1] bach?' asked Beth. Sarah felt her heart leap, but hesitated. She knew she would be expected back as soon as possible to get on with the next job. But it would be so lovely just to sit and talk to another young person, so she flung caution to the winds and said, 'Thank you, that would be lovely.'

The kitchen at Y Dyffryn was calm and quiet, much like the one at Fferm Fach but without the constant noise and clamour of a young family. A grandfather clock ticked peacefully against the far wall, the fire glowed and a tabby cat dozed in front of it. A black kettle was coming to the boil. 'It's lovely here,' said Sarah with a sigh, sinking down into a rocking chair with a patchwork cushion.

Beth shot her a keen look as she took a tea caddy down from a shelf. 'Work you hard, do they, bach?'

Sarah was suddenly conscious of her rough, chapped hands, reddened by much contact with salt and water. She put them into her lap and nodded. 'There's a lot to do.'

---

1. Bara brith is a type of Welsh sweet bread, loaded with currants.

Beth put a slice of bara brith on a willow patterned plate. 'Yes, and I'm thinking Eira Hughes is not the softest of employers, with all those children and the old lady to look after.' She poured tea into a cup, handed it to Sarah and poured another for herself.

Sarah felt her face flush, and then, to her horror, tears came into her eyes. She had grown used to being given orders and sometimes having fault found with her work. Kindness and sympathy didn't often come her way. She had a sudden longing to pour out her heart to this young woman. She took a gulp of tea and said, 'I won't be there forever. It's just that our mam needs the money until our Walter is old enough to get work.'

'Do you see your mam often?'

Sarah shook her head. 'Only once a month or so. She's over in Radnorshire and it's too far to walk there and back in one day when the days are short. The days are pulling out a bit now, though.'

Beth frowned. 'So don't you have time off every week, then?'

'Well, I do, two half-days. But like I said, it's too far to go.'

'So what do you do?'

Sarah shrugged. 'Mostly I just do my mending, or some sewing. Or go for a walk if it's not raining.'

'All by yourself?'

'Yes. I don't mind. I like the quiet.' She did not mention that there were times when she longed for some company, or to spend a whole day at home with her family.

Beth put down her cup and folded her arms. 'Well, next time, why don't you take a walk over this way and come and see me?'

Sarah felt her heart lift again. It would be wonderful just to walk across the fields and spend an afternoon with this friendly young woman. It would be something to look forward to during the days of drudgery, a bright spot in the dreariness of everyday life. She put down her cup and said, 'Oh, that would be wonderful.'

Beth beamed. 'I will enjoy your company too. Glyn always works so hard, and I keep busy, but it's lonely sometimes.' A look of sadness flitted across her face as her eyes went to a corner of the room. Following her gaze, Sarah saw something she had not noticed before – a wooden cradle, like the one Billy had at Fferm Fach, pushed to one side and half-hidden by a Welsh wool blanket folded over it. Beth said softly, 'I had a baby. A little girl, the prettiest thing. Glyn and I thought we were the most blessed people in the world.' She paused, and added quietly, 'She died. Almost two years now and it seems like yesterday.' Tears stood in her eyes.

Faced with the raw grief of the young woman, Sarah did not know what to say. She murmured, 'I'm so sorry. I didn't know.'

Beth seemed to give herself a shake. She said, 'How could you know? It was before you came.' She was thoughtful for a moment, the only sounds the quiet ticking of the clock and the purring of the cat. Then she said suddenly, 'Sarah, do you believe in God?'

Sarah was startled. She'd never been asked a question like that before. She said hesitantly, 'Well, yes. Everyone does, don't they?' She thought of the Bible readings Penry Hughes did every evening, with the little boys fidgeting and the girls looking bored, the grace before meals, the rules for Sundays, the hardness of the chapel pews as the preacher's voice went on and on. The trying to be good. Wasn't all that about believing in God?

Beth put down her teacup. She said, 'I'm not sure I do any more. When our Evie was sick, I prayed and prayed. But she didn't get better. I had to watch her fade and die. God didn't hear, or he didn't answer. People said, "It's God's will," but what kind of God is that? Didn't I pray right? Didn't he hear? Didn't he care? Or maybe he doesn't exist at all!'

The tears were trickling down her cheeks now. Sarah felt rather shocked. She'd never heard anyone talk of God like that before. What on earth would the Hughes family say if they heard? She didn't know what to say. But she reached over, took Beth's hand and squeezed it, and whispered again, 'I'm sorry.'

Beth recovered herself. 'No, it's me who should be sorry, going on like that and you're only young. But I can't talk to Glyn about it. You're a good listener.'

The talk of God had suddenly reminded Sarah that it was Sunday tomorrow, with extra work to be done in preparation. She looked at the grandfather clock and was shocked to see that an hour had passed. She drank the last of her tea quickly and got to her feet. 'I shall have to go. I'm afraid I've stayed too long. Thank you for the tea.'

Beth got up too. 'You're welcome. I've enjoyed your company, and I'm sorry I went on. You will come again, won't you?'

Sarah nodded. 'I will. On my next half-day. Thank you.'

Hurrying home across the fields, Sarah knew she was going to be in trouble. But it was worth it. And she'd go again. They couldn't prevent her in her time off. She would go!

Eight

Sarah expected trouble and she got it. Hurrying home across the fields, she arrived to find a somewhat disorganised household, boys pushing their limits, baby wailing and old Mrs Hughes querulously demanding attention. Alice was setting the table for tea while Nancy washed eggs in the back kitchen. Both looked smug when they saw Sarah.

'Where have you been all this time?' demanded Alice. 'You're in for it now!'

Sarah certainly was, as she discovered when Eira came in, breathless from bringing in the cows for milking and feeding the pig. She dumped down the empty pigswill bucket with a loud clatter. 'Oh, you're back! And not before time, either. That's the last time I'll send you on an errand! And where's the basket, pray?'

In her hurry, Sarah had quite forgotten the empty basket. Still in a fluster, she said, 'I must have left it. I'm sorry. I didn't notice the time –'

'I expected you straight back! I don't pay you to loiter about visiting. We're all behind with everything now. Oh, and there's Penry coming in for his tea and nothing ready. Don't stand there, girl, move!'

Sarah was kept busy until bedtime, catching up with all the extra things to be done on a Saturday. The minimum of cooking was carried out on the Sabbath, so meat must be baked, boiled or roasted the day before to be eaten cold, the vegetables peeled, pudding made, and a row of Sunday boots cleaned and polished. And then there was the weekly bathing, the heating of water to fill the tin bathtub, and smaller children to be scrubbed one by one in front of the kitchen fire while the rest of the family sat in the parlour and listened to the complaining of the old lady.

Sarah was exhausted by the time she sank into bed. But it had all been worth it.

Sunday morning was always a scramble to get the essential farm and dairy work done, the household fed, the old lady attended to, the little boys and baby forced into their best Sunday clothes. The old lady in particular was extra grumpy on the Sabbath.

'Why can't the girl stay with me?' she grumbled. Sarah tried to stifle the urge to remind old Mrs Hughes that she had a name and was not just 'the girl'. 'It's not right, leaving a helpless old lady like me all on her own. What if I had a turn? You'd all be sorry if you found me dead when you got back!'

Eira was briskly efficient with her mother-in-law and did not give in to this kind of talk.

'Sarah goes with us,' she said crisply. 'We are responsible for her religious welfare while she's in this house. You won't have a turn, Mother. We'll be home for dinner.'

Sarah knew old Mrs Hughes was not nearly as helpless as she seemed. She had seen the old lady get out of bed and move around the room quite nimbly when she thought no one was looking. Her daughter-in-law had once told Sarah, in a burst of confidence over the washtub, that old Mrs Hughes had, like many other farm wives, led a hard life, and as soon as her children were gone and her youngest had a wife, she had made up her mind that she would work no more. Over the years, she had convinced herself, and those around her, that she was a helpless invalid.

It was a mile or more's walk across the hillside to get to the chapel. All of them were in their Sunday best and polished boots, with baby William wrapped in a fringed shawl of Welsh wool that covered both mother and baby. Sarah loved this time of freedom, the fresh air, the bleating of the sheep, the signs of life. As they neared the chapel, other worshippers, with Sunday clothes and serious faces could be seen coming, some on foot, those living further afield with ponies and traps, and a few on horseback. A stable block stood beside the chapel for the accommodation of horses, and in the field surrounding the little chapel building, grey headstones marked the graves of past worshippers. A spreading hazel tree by the gate showed bright green leaves, with the first hint of tiny green buds that would be May blossom. Neighbours greeted one another with muted Sunday voices. Most of the men carried Bibles in their work-worn hands. There was some shuffling, coughing, clearing of throats as they filed inside and took their places, but no more talking, not even a whisper.

Sarah noticed, as they sat down in their accustomed places, that Beth and her husband were sitting across from them on the other side of the aisle. Beth turned and gave her a smile, and she felt her heart lift. Beside her on either side, the two little boys fidgeted and squirmed, but did not dare to utter a sound. The Lord's Day and his house must be observed with due reverence.

Sarah found her mind wandering when the sermon was being preached. The visiting preacher, in black, had a long, sad face with deep wrinkles and seemed intent on making the congregation feel guilty for their failings. 'Be not deceived; God is not mocked: for whatsoever a man soweth, that shall he also reap' was his text,[2] delivered in suitably doom-laden tones. The congregation, mainly farming people well-accustomed to the rhythms of sowing and reaping, looked down and shuffled their feet, no doubt remembering their own sins or feeling complacent for their lack of them, according to their natures. The theme of the message seemed to be the strict observance of the Lord's Day, the need to apply themselves to scriptural values and obey the rules. Sarah's attention wandered further; this teaching was not new to her and she heard a version of it every day back at the farm too. She stole a look at Beth, sitting with her husband across the aisle. Beth sat with her eyes downcast, giving no indication of what she might be thinking. Remembering their conversation, Sarah smiled a little. She wondered what thoughts were going through the minds of the other worshippers.

Then she became aware of Eira Hughes' eyes on her, and wiped the smile from her face. Worshipping the Lord was not a laughing matter and the Sabbath should be an occasion of solemnity.

After the last hymn had been sung, the benediction pronounced and the congregation were filing out, the

2. Galatians 6:7, KJV.

atmosphere lightened somewhat. Outside the door, Beth approached with the basket which had held duck eggs, and now contained a large fruit cake wrapped in greaseproof paper. She handed it to Eira and said, 'I'm so sorry I forgot this, Mrs Hughes. I did some baking yesterday evening and I thought you might like this cake.'

Eira visibly softened at the sight of the cake. Baking was something she herself fitted in whenever she had the time. The two women chatted amicably for a few minutes about how the broody hen was settling, about other household matters and the planting of their gardens. Beth seemed to make a point of not speaking to Sarah, which was a relief but also gave her a slightly hurt feeling. She'd thought she might have found a friend in Beth.

She was reassured when, as they were about to go their separate ways, Beth turned her head a little towards Sarah and closed one eye in a broad wink.

CHAPTER

Nine

Amy, present day

Amy awoke with a start. She had been in a deep sleep and dreaming. There was a thumping sound nearby. She groaned and began to struggle out of bed for the start of another hard-working day.

Emily appeared at the bedroom door, dressed in her oldest jeans and hoodie.

'Wake up, Ames! You've overslept again.'

Still half-asleep, Amy asked, 'What's that noise? Is it old Mrs Hughes?'

Emily looked puzzled. 'Who's old Mrs Hughes? You're still dreaming! That's Dad, he reckons we've got mud all over the car and he's banging the floor mats on the garden wall.' She frowned. 'What's the matter? Did you have a nightmare again?'

Amy was searching for her clothes. She said, 'I don't think so. I was dreaming, though.' She pulled on a sock and paused, trying to remember. 'I think it was about Sarah.' The dream was fading fast.

'You're obsessed with her, if you ask me,' said Emily. 'Hurry up! Dad says we're going pony trekking.'

Amy sighed. It would be nice to be consulted about plans for the day now and then.

All the same, the idea of pony trekking appealed to her. Apart from one or two short treks on other holidays, she'd never done much riding.

The pony trekking centre was just a short distance away. With a small group of other trekkers, they were given a brief talk for novice riders, clothing checked for suitability, and given riding helmets. Then, suitably mounted on sturdy Welsh cobs, the group was guided out of the yard and onto the lower slopes of the mountain. Amy felt her spirits rise. She liked the feel of the muscular brown pony she rode, liked the smell of horses and fresh clean air, and the little snorts and grunts of their mounts. The ponies were surefooted, born and bred in the hills and knowing instinctively the route they were taking, having travelled it many times before. It was a beautiful spring morning after an early mist; above them, a skylark rose from the heather and sent its bubbling song back to earth. Sheep grazed placidly on the short turf and took no notice of the riders.

Round the towering height of the Twmpa, they wound their way, travelling across the slope until the guide began to lead them gently uphill to where the road passed through the foothills. Amy's spirits lifted higher. There was a feeling of peace, of being away from the bustle and trials of life, just themselves and their mounts and the natural world under a wide sky. She drew in deep breaths of the clear air.

When they reached the road, they followed it for a while, keeping to the sides when the occasional car passed by. There seemed to be an unspoken code regarding horses and riders; most drivers slowed almost to a crawl when they passed, and were acknowledged by a wave and nod from the guide. When they reached the gap between the two mountain giants, Hay Bluff on their left and the Twmpa on the right, they were ushered off the road and onto a patch of grass beside it. They dismounted, horses rested, and their guide, a young woman in her thirties called Rhian, gave them a little informative talk on the location.

'This is called the Gospel Pass,' she told them. 'It's actually the highest mountain pass in Wales. The name dates back to the time of the Welsh Revival, when hundreds of people in the Welsh valleys were gripped by a wave of religious fervour and their lives were dramatically changed. There was a preacher called Evan Roberts who was one of the leaders, I believe. Suddenly, the miners and their families saw huge changes, not only in their church or chapel-going, but also in the way they lived their lives. Men stopped drinking heavily and some of the pubs had to close for lack of business. Even the pit ponies, used to being hit and sworn at by the miners, were bewildered and hardly knew how to work under the new kindness that was shown them.'

Amy could see that many of the group had not heard any of this before. There were murmurings of surprise and interest. She'd never heard much about the Welsh Revival herself. She could almost see her dad's ears pricking up, and guessed he'd be looking up historical details of this event when they got back to the cottage.

Rhian continued, 'The people from the valleys wanted to share more widely what had happened. They started to send their preachers out into the wider world. One of the ways they got to England was through this pass in the mountains, carrying the gospel message. Another theory dates back much further, to the time of St Paul, who is said to have come here to share the gospel, and that's how it got its name.' She shrugged. 'You can choose which version you like, I suppose.'

First informative lecture over, they remounted and rode through the pass. Before them, the road wended its way through heather-clad slopes on the right, and on the left, a vista of green hills and hollows lay before them. In one of the hollows, a lone hawthorn, sheltered from the harsh winter winds and storms, would soon be a mass of creamy-white blossom. After a while, they drew aside into one of the hollows and dismounted again to let the horses graze on the short grass and to eat their own packed lunches. Rhian told them that if they followed the road for several miles, it would eventually take them to the Welsh valleys in one direction, or on the other, over the border into England.

'There are some fascinating places further on,' she said. 'Little villages and hamlets tucked away in folds and dips. And there's Llanthony Abbey at Capel-y-Ffin, in ruins now but with a history all its own. In the nineteenth century, there was a devout Catholic monk called Father Ignatius whose ambition was to restore the monastic life in Britain. He founded a community at Llanthony and was responsible for building the Abbey, or the Priory, as it's officially called.'

Interested in spite of herself, Amy tried to digest the unfamiliar place names and their history. She found she was quite disappointed when Rhian paused for breath, and then said, 'We won't go any further today, but Llanthony is definitely worth a visit. Not now, though. I think we'll all be saddle-sore enough tomorrow after our ride today.' She grinned.

She was right about the saddle-soreness. By the time they had gone the allotted distance and made their way home, stiffness was already setting in.

Dad groaned. 'I think there'll be a queue for the bath tonight! Do we have plenty of bath salts?'

Mum assured him that they had, and even Amy had to admit she couldn't wait for a long hot soak. Mum continued, 'We'll have to go easy on the water, though; I think the supply is limited sometimes. Never mind, the stiffness will wear off, and we've had a great day, haven't we?'

Nobody argued with that. 'Just the same, I can't wait to get back to the lambing tomorrow,' said Emily.

And maybe I'll go to Y Dyffryn too, thought Amy. *Maybe I can have a look at those old papers Ceri mentioned. Perhaps I'll find out a little bit more about Sarah.*

Her heart gave a little skip of anticipation.

CHAPTER

Ten

There'd been a change in the weather overnight. The summit of the mountain was hidden in a cloud of mist, with wisps and trails reaching down the slopes. A group of shapes moved through the mist, too large for sheep.

'Ponies,' said Emily, joining Amy at the window. 'They run wild on the mountain most of the summer, but they're brought down to be fed in the winter.'

'Brrr, looks chilly,' said Mum. 'I think I'm going to light the wood burner and have a nice cosy day inside.'

All of them were stiff and sore after yesterday's trekking, but Dad announced his intention of taking a brisk walk and then doing some work.

'A good day for revision?' he suggested, with a sideways look at Emily and Amy.

Both girls quickly thought of other things to do. 'I'm going to Y Dyffryn,' said Emily. 'Whatever the weather, the lambs keep coming.'

'Me too,' said Amy, in case her parents thought of some other tasks.

'As long as you don't get in the way,' said Dad. They assured him they would not.

'Be back for lunch,' said Mum, consulting the contents of the fridge. 'I think it's the kind of day for a hearty stew.'

'Thank goodness they've got things to occupy them,' said Emily, as they set off across the field. Amy found herself almost giggling, which didn't happen much these days. Emily sounded so much like a parent herself.

They were greeted at Y Dyffryn by the usual loud chorus of furious barking, which quickly turned to waving tails and welcoming doggy grins.

Emily was delighted. 'They know us already!'

David and Ceri seemed pleased to see them too. 'Five more new lambs in the night,' said David. 'I didn't get much shut-eye, I can tell you.'

He did look tired, standing at the Rayburn and slurping coffee, not even sitting down. Greatly daring, Emily said, 'Why don't you have a proper rest and I'll go and check on the ewes? I can always come back for you if there's a problem.'

David said, 'You know, I think I will. Thanks. Just for a few minutes.'

Emily left with the dogs. David sat down in the cushioned chair by the Rayburn, and within seconds his eyes were closed and he was faintly snoring. Ceri grinned, looking at Amy and put her finger to her lips. 'Poor love, he's exhausted. Your sister's a Godsend. Let's leave him to sleep as long as he can. Come into the sitting room.'

The sitting room was a little smaller than the kitchen and not quite as warm. A fire was laid in the grate but not lit. Well-worn but comfy-looking chairs and a sofa were grouped around it, and Amy thought it must be very cosy in the winter with a roaring fire. Then her eyes widened as she saw a table at the back of the room, with a battered old suitcase and a dusty cardboard box beside it. The lid of the box was open, and inside were papers and envelopes with handwriting on them. Could this be the old material that had come from Fferm Fach?

Ceri smiled. 'I brought them down from the attic, haven't had time to look at them yet. Thought you might like to have a rummage. Shall I light the fire for you?'

'Oh, no – no, thank you,' stammered Amy. 'It's fine. I'll keep my coat on.'

'I'll leave you to it, then,' said Ceri. 'I'd better get on with my jobs. I hope David will sleep for a while. I'll go and check on your sister in a bit.' She pulled out a chair and motioned Amy to sit down at the table.

Amy felt quite overwhelmed. 'Doesn't David mind?' she asked. 'There might be personal things in there – letters and stuff.'

'David doesn't mind a bit,' said Ceri. 'I think he's glad to see a young person who's not staring at a screen the whole time. Happy hunting!'

She left, closing the door softly. Amy opened the case and looked at the reams of stuff piled higgledy-piggledy inside. Where to start? She took a deep breath and began to investigate. There were lots of envelopes, mostly handwritten, some typed in a businesslike way, with clear windows. There were other papers too, brochures for animal remedies, NFU pamphlets, some postcards, receipts, invoices. The first few envelopes she opened were bills for animal feed, the vet and farm tools. Then she found a handwritten letter on black-edged paper, which turned out to be a letter of condolence for a bereavement. There were others with black-edged stationery. Amy put them all together in a pile to be looked at later, the business letters in another pile. They were interesting too. *How little things cost then*, she thought wonderingly. An axe-handle, two shillings, which she worked out would be 10p in today's money. Repairs to a binder, which she guessed was some kind of machinery, ten shillings, or 50p.

But she pulled herself up short. The bills and letters were all addressed to members of the family, no business of hers. What she was looking for was some reference to Sarah Rees, some clue as to who she had been and what had happened to her.

Amy was vaguely aware of time passing and her fingers and toes getting colder, but hardly noticed. There seemed to be mountains of papers in the dusty suitcase. She pushed it aside and thought she'd try the cardboard box.

As soon as she began, she saw there was a difference in the contents. The same mixture of letters and other stuff, the seed catalogues, the vet's bills, the adverts for sheep and cattle ailments. But the letters here were addressed to Mr P. Hughes, Esquire, or sometimes to Mr and Mrs P. Hughes. These must have come from Fferm Fach when David's family bought it. Her heart gave a skip of excitement. This was the family Sarah had lived with. Maybe there'd be something more about her here.

She opened a few of the letters. Nothing much of interest, mostly details of a death in the wider family, or a child's illness, or other bits of everyday news, like the new goslings hatching or a bumper crop of apples. There seemed to be larger items at the bottom of the box. She rummaged down and pulled out some school exercise books, shabby and dog-eared, but there were names on the covers. Alice

Hughes, Nancy Hughes. *None for the younger children,* she thought. Then she remembered that the younger ones would probably have used slates.

She was opening the first book, belonging to Nancy, which seemed to be very ordinary lists of spellings, with an essay or two, when a thought struck her. How had she known the younger children would use slates? How would she have known there were young children in the family at all?

Amy stopped her rummaging and sat perfectly still for a moment. Had these details been part of the dreams she'd been having? They seemed so clear in her mind, and yet the dreams had quickly faded, as most dreams do.

'Amy?' She hadn't noticed Ceri opening the door and putting her head round it. A savoury smell of something cooking came in with her, it smelled like cottage pie. Amy was suddenly hungry. Whatever time was it?

'You seemed to be in another world,' said Ceri. 'Found something interesting? Only they've come in from the lambing shed, and Emily says you're meant to be home for lunch. Your mum phoned her.'

Amy had switched off her own phone. She looked at her watch. Almost two hours had passed.

'Oh gosh, sorry,' she said. 'I forgot the time.'

Ceri smiled. 'It's OK. You can come back another day if you like. It's been a good morning. David had a long nap and three more lambs have arrived safely. I'm sure Emily will be coming again.'

Amy got up and began to tidy away the papers, realising from the stiffness of her arms and legs that she had sat for a long time. It was only when she was replacing the exercise books in the box that something else caught her eye. Another smaller notebook was there, and on its cover was the name Sarah Rees.

'Are you OK, Amy?' asked Ceri. 'You've gone quite pale. Did you get cold? I should have lit the fire for you.'

Amy pulled herself together. 'No, no, I'm fine, not cold at all. It's this.' She picked up the notebook and held it out. 'It's got Sarah's name on it. Maybe it's a diary or something.'

Ceri took the book. 'Oh, that's interesting. We had no idea what was in those collections. Would you like to take it home to look at?'

'Oh, could I?' said Amy. Her heart was thumping with excitement. Who could tell what secrets might be contained in that little book?

'Sure,' said Ceri. 'You can bring it back next time.'

Emily appeared at the door, her hands red and raw from scrubbing. 'Hurry up, Mum sounded a bit tetchy.'

Amy put the notebook into her jacket pocket. She wanted to read it by herself, preferably in the peace of her room. On the way home, she listened to Emily's chat of breech birth and post-natal prolapse with only half an ear. She wondered what it was that made her so keen to find out more about Sarah Rees. The fact that she was the same age as Sarah had been when she wrote on the bedroom wall? The fact that she was sleeping in Sarah's bedroom?

The fact that they were both unhappy ... That thought made her stop suddenly in the field next to Fferm Fach.

Emily looked at her. 'What's the matter, Ames?'

Amy gave herself a mental shake. 'Oh,' she said. 'I was just thinking.'

'You think too much, if you ask me,' said her sister. 'You need to get out and get more exercise and fresh air. Moping about looking at old stuff isn't good.'

'Yes, Mum,' said Amy. 'Any more advice while you're at it?'

Emily gave her a shove. 'Oh, come on. I'm starving!'

It was a relief later when Mum suggested an early night might be a good idea. They had all been for a long walk that afternoon, and came to a place that overlooked the chapel at Penrheol. Both girls were surprised when Mum said, 'What do you think about going there again this Sunday? It's Easter Sunday, after all. I'd quite like to.'

Nobody disagreed. Amy thought, *I'd like a proper look at those old gravestones.* Emily said, 'Fine with me. I could stop off at Y Dyffryn on the way home.'

Back in her bedroom, Amy took a look at the writing on the wall and compared it to that on the cover of the notebook. It was the same. She got into bed and started to read.

It was a very slim notebook. Amy had the feeling that a large part of it had become detached and was missing. The entries were quite brief and mostly about everyday life on the farm, the hatching of chicks and ducklings and something called 'gulls', which puzzled her. Not seagulls, surely? There were accounts of lambing, numbers of newborns, details of bottle-fed ones, entries about crops planted and the work of the farmhouse, a rare mention or two of a visit to her family, and a joyful account or two of her days off and visiting Beth at Y Dyffryn. The last entry read: 'Good week. Went home for Mothering Sunday, lovely. Then went to see Beth on my half-day. She had a letter from her sister over the border, telling her about something that's happening over there . . .' And there the entry ended, in the middle of the sentence on the last page, leaving Amy wide awake and full of curiosity. Would she be able to find the missing pages among the other letters and papers? She punched her pillows, pulled up the blankets and tried to sleep.

Eleven

Sarah, early 1920s

Mothering Sunday came, chilly with a thin wind but dry overhead. Sarah felt her spirits lift as she scurried through the early morning work. Today, she would get the whole day to visit her mother and her brothers. It would take almost two hours of walking to get there and the same back, but in-between there would be precious time spent with her family.

Here at Fferm Fach, not many concessions were made for the special day; Eira was as hard-worked and careworn as usual, the old lady was querulous. They would have to manage without her as they prepared for another Sunday of best clothes, chapel, Sabbath restrictions and the resultant bad humour. Sarah would have no part in it today. Early work done, she dressed in her best, took her basket and blithely wished them all farewell.

The walk into the town of Hay was pleasant – downhill all the way when she reached the road, marked by the early lambs in the fields and catkins in the hedges. They had already turned into 'lamb's tails', covered with yellow pollen that meant there would be plenty of hazelnuts later. The town itself was quiet, sleeping along the riverbanks, dominated by the ruined castle at its heart. One or two people greeted her with a friendly 'Good morning!' but she didn't slacken her pace, eager not to waste a precious minute. Over the bridge, with the river wide and swift-flowing beneath, uphill for a while, then down again into a quiet village with a grey stone church. Then a smaller road which was suddenly very steep indeed, and a steady climb for two miles or more. Sarah had walked this road from childhood to reach the village, where she'd gone to school, and knew every corner and every turn, every dwelling and farm and gateway, as well as the trees and hedgerows. Here was a thicket of brambles where she'd discovered a thrush's nest one day when she was walking to school. She had been heartbroken when, a day or two later, she found the nest pulled apart and fragments of sky-blue eggshell on the ground. She'd guessed it had been destroyed by some birds-nesting boy with no care for wildlife, and wept at the loss. A little further on, she knew, there would be a bank with a patch of primroses peeping from the grass. She hoped they'd be in bloom, and yes, there they were, like a patch of sunlight. She'd planned to pick a bunch for her mother and did so, bringing them to her face to sniff their delicate scent.

Sarah had just tied the bunch with a length of thread she'd brought along, and placed them carefully in her basket, when she heard the clip-clop of hooves and the grinding of wheels on the surface of the road. Round the corner came a pony and trap, with a man she recognised at the pony's head, Mr Thomas Powell, the owner of a large neighbouring farm and the owner of the cottage tenanted by Sarah's family. He caught up with her and halted the pony.

'Good day, young Sarah! Home to your mam for Mothering Sunday, is it?'

She nodded, guessing by his Sunday suit and tie and polished boots that he had been to the church in the village. Mr Powell had always been reckoned to be a good landlord, expecting his rents on time, but fair and honest as well. Sarah knew that he had given her mother time to collect herself and make the decisions needed when her husband died. Now he said, 'You've a long walk from over the other side. There's a good flat stretch for a bit yet until we reach my gate, and old Ben's had a rest for a spell now. Jump up in the trap and you'll be home all the quicker.'

'Oh, thank you, Mr Powell,' said Sarah, her heart giving a skip as she realised she'd have more time at home. She climbed nimbly into the trap. They set off at a smart clop, the pony realising that home and a good feed were not far away. When they reached the lane to Mr Powell's farm, he turned in without any guidance. The farmer brought him to a halt. 'Whoa, hold up a minute, Ben, and let this young lady get out. There you go, young Sarah. Saved your legs a bit and not far to go now. Remember me to your mam and good day to you.' He touched his cap.

Nearly at her own home now. Just one more corner, and there was the turn to their own cottage. She skipped down the lane with a light heart. There stood the cottage, slate-roofed, and in front of it the patch of garden where Sarah's mother grew vegetables. An apple tree stood near the gate, just beginning to show pink and white blossom; behind was the small field where the cow grazed. Sarah stood for a moment, just taking in the familiar look and feel of the place. Home.

Her mother was a little surprised to see her daughter so early. She was a small woman, her dark hair escaping in tendrils from the kerchief around her head. Sarah noticed with a pang that there were a few grey hairs she had not noticed before. A delicious smell of dinner was in the air and her tummy rumbled. She put down the basket and hugged her mother. 'I had a lift some of the way, Mam. With Mr Powell. How are you keeping? Where are the boys?'

'Ah. He's a kind man. I'm keeping well. The boys are up in the field – they've made new catapults and they're trying to catch rabbits. How are you, love? You'll be tired after that long walk. Sit you down and I'll make a nice cup of tea. I've got a piece of brisket in the pot, and the first rhubarb for a pie.'

Sarah felt tears come to her eyes as she watched her mother bustle about and listened to her chatter. It was an unusual thing for her to be waited on and fussed over. Then she remembered the day. She took the primroses from the basket and presented them, and with them the bundle of notes she had so carefully saved since her last visit. 'Happy Mothering Sunday, Mam.'

Her mother had tears in her eyes too. 'Oh, love, you're such a good daughter! What would I do without you?'

Sarah could not let her mother see her cry. She jumped up and busied herself, finding a glass to put the primroses in, and dipping water from the pail in the corner. She must never let her mother see how difficult her life was. She would only have to stick it out for another year or a bit longer anyway. Until Walter left school and found work.

Over the tea, her mother confided that Graham, the younger boy, was giving her some cause for worry. 'He needs a father's hand, I'm afraid,' she said sadly. 'Headstrong and wilful, he is. Doesn't like school, wants to play about. He could be a good scholar if he put his mind to it. But he'd rather be birds-nesting and catching rabbits and larking about with the boys from the village.'

Sarah tried to console her. 'He's only a boy, Mam. How is Walter?'

Her mother's face lit up. 'Oh, Walter's such a good boy! Getting to be my right hand. The headmaster says he's the brightest in the school, and ought to go on to grammar school.'

Sarah felt her heart lurch. She put down her cup carefully. 'And does he want to?'

'He doesn't say much. But I think he'd have liked the chance. I tell him he's lucky. Mr Powell has a job there, all waiting for him when he leaves school.'

And then it'll be my turn, thought Sarah. But a new idea came into her mind, one that made her heart sink like a stone. Walter was bright. He could go to grammar school. He ought to have the chance. *I ought to give him that chance.*

She gave herself a shake. She wouldn't spoil the day with unhappy thoughts. She was about to change the subject and tell her mother about her new friend, Beth, when there was a clatter of boots at the door. Her two brothers burst in, ruddy-faced from the cold, Graham, ten years old, handsome and fearless, and Walter, thirteen, quieter and had suddenly grown taller since the last time she'd seen him. Suddenly, the quiet little room was filled with noise and energy.

'Sal, you're here already! We been rabbit hunting, nearly caught one too, only just missed him, the blighter!' They brandished their home-made catapults. Sarah couldn't help smiling at their enthusiasm. They were casting glances at her basket, and she produced the sticks of liquorice she'd brought, which they began to chew immediately.

'You'll spoil your dinners!' she warned.

'No danger of that,' said their mother, going back to the pot over the fire. 'Eat me out of house and home they do, the rascals!' She laughed. Suddenly, the little house was full of good cheer and laughter and love. Sarah felt herself relax. She was home, with the ones she loved most in the world. And she knew without a shadow of a doubt that she would do anything, make any sacrifice, to keep her loved ones happy.

CHAPTER

Twelve

Sarah had looked forward greatly to going to see Beth on one of her half-days. The thought of it was a bright spot in the dreary sameness of the days. For a week or two, she kept the thought as a delicious event to savour and anticipate.

The Hughes family seemed to notice a change in her and reacted in their various ways.

'You look like the cat that got the cream,' said old Mrs Hughes sourly, on a morning when she declared her rheumatics had kept her awake all night. 'I can't see what there is to be grinning about.'

'It's such a lovely day,' said Sarah. 'The sun is shining and the birds are singing!'

'Nice for those who can enjoy it,' said Mrs Hughes grumpily.

The younger Mrs Hughes was not so keen on the sunshine. 'Shows up the dirty windows something terrible! And the cobwebs – I can see we'll have to get to the spring cleaning before long, Sarah.'

Even the thought of the spring cleaning to come could not dampen Sarah's mood.

Alice was convinced that Sarah had a young man and constantly quizzed her about it. 'Who is it? It's a wonder you found anyone halfway decent around here! Where did you meet him? Go on, Sarah, tell us!'

'There's nothing to tell,' said Sarah.

She visited Beth on an afternoon when there had been a shower of rain overnight, the lambs were coming, duck and hen eggs hatching and life was busier than ever, but she relished her afternoon of freedom. She didn't care if the family found out she was visiting Beth either. On her way across the fields, she picked a bright bunch of cowslips, violets and stitchwort and presented it to Beth.

Beth buried her face in the flowers. 'Oh, how lovely! I love wildflowers, so much nicer than prim and proper old gilly-flowers and daffs and such.'

The kitchen was as peaceful as before, the cat curled up on the rocking chair, the grandfather clock ticking. Beth made tea and sat down opposite Sarah. 'Now, tell me what you've been up to.'

'Well, I went to see Mam and my brothers on Mothering Sunday,' said Sarah. 'That was lovely. Since then, it's just been the usual.' She tried not to pull a face. They drank their tea and talked about the seasonal work on the farm, while a sudden April shower lashed against the window.

Beth drained her cup and got to her feet. 'Sorry to rush you, but it's a busy time here too. Chicks, geese, ducks all hatching. By the way, you must tell Eira Hughes the duck eggs she sent have all hatched, every one. It's the gulls who are coming now, and they have to be watched. The shower's over now. Coming?'

Sarah pulled on her coat and they went out together. In the rickyard, two fussy mother hens clucked and fretted over their broods, their clucks changing to a high calling note that brought the chicks running whenever they discovered some tasty morsel. The hen with the ducklings seemed sadly perplexed by the behaviour of her own young, who eagerly splashed into every fresh puddle they discovered, flapping their tiny wings and enjoying the water hugely. Sarah couldn't help laughing as their anxious mother fussed up and down. The hen had no liking for water herself, preferring a refreshing dust bath.

The geese were not quite as entertaining. A furious hissing came from a coop within their enclosure. 'The old gander's in there,' said Beth. 'He goes crazy whenever there are gullies hatching, thinks everyone is after his young and he has to protect them. I have to keep him shut up. Don't go near the coop. He's quite likely to stick his head through the bars and nip the backs of your legs.'

Sarah kept her distance. The gander at Fferm Fach was unpredictable too, and respected no one but Eira Hughes, who carried a stout stick with her whenever tending them. The mother of the hatchlings was cross too, hissing a warning as Beth approached her. Sarah made sure to stand well back. Three goslings had already emerged, small greeny-yellow balls of fluff, cheeping sleepily and cuddling into their mother's downy breast feathers. Two more of the large eggs had little holes in them, and in one, Sarah could see a tiny beak pecking away at the shell from inside. Another had just split its shell and emerged wet and bedraggled. Beth quickly picked it out of the broken shell.

'Another one safe and sound,' she said. 'Sweet little things, aren't they? I hate to think of them ending up as Christmas dinners, but that's the way it is.'

Sarah gave a shudder, remembering last year's preparations of those Christmas dinners at Fferm Fach. The December week of slaughter, limp bodies to be plucked in the back kitchen, carefully saving the feathers for pillows and bolsters, taking care no blood was dripped on them to spoil them. Even the wings had to be saved for brushing the hearths. The fine down got everywhere, tickling noses and sticking to hair and eyelashes, spreading throughout the house however hard one tried to contain them. The dressing was even worse, steaming innards to be removed, singeing off any remaining fluff, the legs and wings arranged just so and finished with a sprig of parsley. Sarah was thankful that Eira did not entrust her with the job of dressing geese for market, but the feathering was bad enough.

They finished their tour of the poultry pens and left the mothers to settle back on their nests, and the gander to hiss with frustration at not being able to defend them. The sun had come out again as they crossed the yard, and there was the soft clip-clop of hooves approaching.

'Oh, the postman!' said Beth.

The elderly grey-haired man rummaged through his saddlebag. 'A letter for you today, missus,' he said, handing down a white envelope. 'And good day to you, ladies.' He touched his cap and rode out of the yard.

Beth scanned the envelope, recognising the handwriting. 'Oh, it's from my cousin Joan, over at Michaelchurch Escley. I wonder what she's got to say. I haven't heard from her for a long time. Let's go inside and find out.'

CHAPTER
Thirteen

The kettle was singing on the hob. Beth made tea, and while they were drinking it, she slit open the envelope and read the letter. Afterwards she seemed deep in thought.

'Not bad news, I hope?' ventured Sarah.

Beth seemed to pull herself back into the present. 'No, not bad news. It's an invitation really.' She paused. 'As I said, Joan lives at Michaelchurch Escley, over on the other side of the mountain. It's ten miles or so. I've only been there once, when I was a child.'

The name was unfamiliar to Sarah. 'Is that a farm?'

'No, Michaelchurch is a village. They're farming people, though, like most of us. Joan's husband works as a farrier, I believe. She's asked me to go and visit. It would mean staying the night – too far to get there and back in one day.'

'Will you go?'

Beth was thoughtful again. 'In a way, I'd love to. I haven't spent a night away for a long time. It's a busy time, but I know Glyn wouldn't stop me from going. Besides, another week or two and most of the lambs will have come.'

Sarah felt a little twinge of envy. How lovely to visit a new place and even spend a night! 'Perhaps you could go when it's less busy.'

Beth shook her head. 'No, there's something else. There are some special meetings she wants me to go to with her, in the village. This preacher,' she consulted the letter, 'Stephen Jeffreys, he's coming from South Wales. Used to be a miner, she says.' She paused again. 'The thing is, as I told you, I don't believe in God any more. I don't know that it's my kind of thing. I go to chapel with Glyn, but, well—' She picked up a spoon and stirred her tea absently. 'Then again, maybe this fellow has something different to say. Maybe I ought to give him a chance. And I'd love to see Joan.' She put down the teaspoon and looked at Sarah. 'I think I will go. I'll have to talk to Glyn first and then I'll write back. '

Sarah had been thinking about that long journey, twice the length she had to travel to see her own family. 'It will be a long walk.'

'I wouldn't walk,' said Beth. 'I'd take the pony.' She drained her teacup and set it down suddenly as a new idea seemed to come to her. 'Sarah, why don't you come with me? You could take my pony and I'd ride Glyn's!' She clasped her hands together, eyes shining. 'Oh, it would be fun! And Joan wouldn't mind you staying too, she's a friendly body.'

Sarah felt a wave of longing. How wonderful to spend a whole couple of days with her new friend, out in the fresh air, riding across the mountain, seeing a new place. She said sadly, 'But I have to work. Mrs Hughes would never let me have the time off.'

'Wouldn't she? What if you offered to work on your half-days for two or three weeks, and save up your free time? You could ask her really nicely, and I could ask too, say I really need someone with me. Let's try at least!'

A small flicker of hope rose in Sarah. Would it, could it, be possible? She made up her mind, there and then, that she would try, choose a moment when Mrs Hughes was in a good mood. She really had nothing to lose.

The moment came sooner than she had expected. Mrs Hughes did not often go to market these days; in fact, she had not been at all since the birth of Billy. This week, however, she decided that she would venture forth. The hens were laying again, and there was a surplus of eggs to be sold, the cow had a young calf and Eira Hughes and Sarah had made several pounds of butter that week with the fresh milk. Some of it could be taken to market. She also decided she would kill and dress a couple of hens that were no longer the best of layers. All for the Thursday market day. Her husband would ride in with her.

'You won't have too much to do, with the children at school,' Mrs Hughes told Sarah briskly as they loaded produce into the panniers. 'Just the baby and the old lady. Billy's tooth is through, so he'll be no trouble.'

Sarah looked doubtfully at Billy, at that moment blissfully asleep in his cradle. It wouldn't last, she knew. Billy's naps never did. He would wake and scream for his mother, and goodness knows what would happen when he found her gone.

'We'll be back before dark,' promised Mrs Hughes. Sarah watched them ride away down the lane with a sinking feeling.

She was right about Billy. He woke and fretted and whined, and finally took to loud wailing. Old Mrs Hughes complained from her room about the noise. It was too early for his bottle, so finally Sarah wrapped him in a shawl and wrapped the shawl about herself too, as she'd seen mothers do, and carried him with her while she went about her tasks. It seemed a long day. The children were home before their parents returned and were in tiresome moods, the boys bickering and fighting and the girls argumentative. Sarah had hoped Alice would help, at least with the baby, but she didn't, saying she had a headache and flouncing up to her room.

Sarah's own head was aching by the time Mr and Mrs Hughes returned. She had never felt so tired, with the work she'd done and the weight of responsibility for the household she had carried. Mrs Hughes, on the other hand, seemed greatly refreshed by the outing and the change. The produce had made a good price and she had enjoyed some talk with other farmers' wives. She had bought sweets for the children, cough drops for her mother-in-law and shop cakes for them all. She also handed a small paper bag of sweets to Sarah, pleased to find everything shipshape, the fire bright, kettle singing and table laid. 'You did well,' she said, a rare word of praise, to which Sarah did not quite know how to reply.

Alice came down the stairs, showing signs of just having awoken from a nap. 'Tell us about the shops, Mam,' she begged. 'And what people were wearing. Were there any of the new fashions?'

Her mother began to remove her hat and coat, and sniffed. 'If by new fashions you mean those dreadful short haircuts, yes, I saw a few. And even some of the short skirts that seem to be coming in. Disgracefully short, some of them, almost up to the knees!' She smoothed down her own ankle-length skirt and picked up her apron, giving her daughter a keen look. 'And you can take that smirk off your face too, miss. No daughter of mine will be wearing anything so immodest, so don't think you will! I hope you've been making yourself useful and helping Sarah.'

Alice didn't answer, but gave Sarah a sideways look. Mrs Hughes continued, 'Sarah has done well and she's looking tired, so she can rest this evening and you two girls do the jobs. Won't hurt you, great girls like you. You take Billy and give him his bottle now, Alice.'

Alice shot a look of resentment at Sarah as she handed over the baby. A new thought came suddenly to Sarah that made her catch her breath. Was this the opportunity she'd been waiting for? Taking her courage in both hands, she asked, 'Mrs Hughes, do you think I could have a couple of days off? I'd work my usual half-days, or more, to make up.'

Mrs Hughes looked surprised. Sarah had never made such a request before. Sarah held her breath, expecting a refusal. But Mrs Hughes said, 'You want to spend a bit of time with your family, is that it? Is your mam not well?'

Sarah gulped. 'No, it's not that. Beth – Mrs Parry – has asked me to go with her to visit her cousin over at Michaelchurch Escley.' She paused, and went on, 'There's some meetings she wants to go to, some preacher from South Wales, and she wants company.'

She wondered if she'd given too much information, because Mrs Hughes frowned disapprovingly. 'What does she want with going all that way to hear preaching? Isn't our chapel good enough?'

Sarah didn't reply. She clasped her hands, red and chapped from hard work. She might have known she'd never get permission. But the good humour of the day had not left her employer, at least not yet. She said, 'Well, you have shown willing and done well today. You can go, this once. But don't make a habit of it, mind.'

Fourteen

The morning came when Sarah was to have her big adventure. She was up early and nothing could dampen her mood, the grumblings of the old lady, wranglings of the children, or the harassed looks of Mrs Hughes, who Sarah suspected was already having a few misgivings about granting her the time off. Sarah had already worked through some of her half-days, and Eira could not change her mind now. Sarah laid the fire before she left, took in tea to the old lady and then she was off, with her few possessions for overnight packed in her carpet bag.

It was a sparkling morning, dew on the grass, a light mist already rising upwards as she sped across the fields to Y Dyffryn. She had never been on a journey this far away before. When she lived at home, her world had consisted of their little house near a Radnorshire village, the daily walks to the village school, church on Sundays and the very occasional trip to visit a relative who would be just a mile or two away. Coming to Fferm Fach, crossing the river into another county had seemed like a great adventure, but once there, any further travel had been limited to Sunday chapel across the mountain, the occasional long walk home, the even more rare visit to the market town on the banks of the river. Truth to tell, Sarah found the town of Hay a little scary. So many people, most of them strangers, so many bleating sheep when it was sheep sales time, lowing cattle herded into market pens, ponies, horses, traps and farm wagons. Motor cars were beginning to appear, frightening things that made a lot of noise and travelled at great speeds. She had been honked at more than once when one of those machines appeared just as she was trying to cross the road.

But this was different. This would be just Beth and herself, on horseback, riding across the mountain and crossing the border, not just into another county but another country, from Wales to England. Her heart was beating fast with excitement.

Beth had the ponies saddled and bridled, waiting in the yard. She hurried from the house with a basket on her arm. 'Oh, you're here! That's good, we can make an early start. I've got plenty of food for the journey, and some fresh eggs and butter for Joan. Have you ridden a pony before?'

Sarah had to confess she had not. Her family had never owned a pony, and there was no opportunity for riding at Fferm Fach. Her journeys had always been on foot except for the rare times she had ridden in the trap.

'Never mind,' said Beth briskly. 'I'll help you mount and dismount, and just follow what I do when you're up there. Peggy is a quiet little creature, aren't you, my love?' She stroked the velvety nose of the grey pony, and the pony snuffled and nuzzled her hand.

Beth helped Sarah into the saddle, showing her how to put her left foot in the stirrup, swing the right leg over and arrange her skirts. She mounted nimbly herself, and waved to her husband, who had appeared from one of the buildings at the sound of their voices.

'You go careful now,' he called. 'Give my regards to Joan and Ifor, and I'll see you back tomorrow. Safe journey!'

'It's so good of him to let me go,' said Beth as they rode together out of the yard and onto the rough mountain track. 'Most of the lambs have come now, but he'll have to see to the fowls and everything else. Still some gulls to hatch but he knows what to do. He's so good.'

They rode in silence for a while, Sarah concentrating hard on getting used to the gait of the pony and the feeling of being a distance from the ground.

'You won't fall off,' said Beth, guessing her thoughts. 'Just leave it to Peggy and enjoy the ride.'

After a while, Sarah began to feel that she was indeed enjoying it. Peggy was sure-footed on the mountain turf, having travelled it many times before. They climbed the slope of the foothills, covered with heather and whinberry bushes until they reached a spot where they could look down on Y Dyffryn and Fferm Fach nestled below, and other farms spread across the slopes, and the grey building of Penrheol Chapel. The sun was rising in the sky, white clouds scudded across the blue, baby lambs called to their mothers and a gentle breeze caressed the cheeks of the riders. Nothing to be done but let the sturdy ponies carry them along.

They climbed until they reached a place where the roadway wended its way round the base of Hay Bluff on the left, with the even higher peak of the Twmpa to the right. Here they rested the ponies for a while after their climb, before taking the road between the two mountains, which

Beth said was called the Gospel Pass. Riding through the narrow pass, with the two mountains towering on either side, Sarah couldn't help wondering about the name. 'Why is it called the Gospel Pass?'

'I believe it's to do with the revival that happened down in the Welsh valleys at the turn of the century,' said Beth. 'Twenty or more years ago now. Suddenly, all the churches and chapels down there had some kind of religious experience, so I've been told. The preachers used to come up here to talk about it.' She paused for a moment. 'Come to think of it, this Stephen Jeffreys we're going to hear may have had something to do with it. Joan did mention something.'

Sarah pondered this for a moment. Then a thought occurred to her. Beth had said she didn't believe in God any more, and she seemed to blame him for the loss of her baby. And she'd implied she only went to chapel to please her husband. Sarah had puzzled over this. How could you blame someone if you didn't believe they existed? And why, then, was Beth so anxious to take this trip to hear more preaching about God? Sarah wasn't quite brave enough to ask. She put the thought away and made up her mind just to enjoy it all and not ask questions.

On the other side of the pass, new vistas opened up before them. The road wound on through gentle green hills and deep valleys, twisting and turning to avoid the rocky outcrops they passed. Sheep grazed on the new grass. In a sheltered hollow, a small hawthorn tree was a mass of creamy-white buds.

'Oh, that's so pretty!' she exclaimed.

Beth nodded. 'I love the may blossom. You should see it when it's out fully! Too rough and windy for many trees, especially down over our side, but that one's found a sheltered place to root itself.'

This side of the mountain seemed gentler altogether. Occasionally they dipped down into valleys where there were thick clusters of trees, rowans and hawthorn and beech, or a stream that gushed down the hillside. At one wooded spot, they saw the unmistakable shape of a fox come out from a cluster of bushes, lope in a leisurely way across the road in front of them, and disappear into trees on the other side. There were nesting birds too; on one tall mountain ash, a blackbird perched and poured out his beautiful song.

They stopped at a grassy place beside a roadside stream where the horses could drink, and dismounted to eat their lunch. The ponies drank deeply and grazed on the young grass. Sarah gave a sigh of content. 'It's so beautiful! I wish we could stay here forever.'

Beth sighed too. 'I see what you mean. But then, I'd be missing my Glyn, wouldn't I?' She laughed and began to gather together the picnic things. 'We'd better get on. We want to get to Michaelchurch in plenty of time to see Joan before the meeting.'

During the afternoon, Sarah began to feel she'd been riding forever. Her muscles were aching and she knew she'd be very stiff tomorrow. *But it's all worth it*, she reminded herself firmly.

They passed by farms, some of which had sheepdogs that barked at the travellers riding by, and then a village that Beth said was called Craswall. 'Not far now,' she said. 'Just another few miles.'

Those last few miles seemed the longest of all, thought Sarah. But at last Beth pointed forwards and said, 'We're nearly there! Look, you can just see the church tower.' And then, round the corner was the village, a group of dwellings clustered on the banks of the River Escley, which gave the place its name. And, standing out against the green of the background, there was also a large white tent pitched in a field beside the road.

'If I'm not mistaken,' said Beth. 'That is where the meetings will be.'

CHAPTER
Fifteen

Beth's cousin proved to be a large, cheerful, friendly person, who welcomed Beth with open arms and gave Sarah a warm hug too.

'Beth told me about you. You're very welcome here, my lovely.'

Joan's husband, Ifor, was small and wiry, as quiet and retiring as his wife was talkative and inquisitive. But both of them gave a warm welcome to the two travellers. The kettle was singing on the hob and the table laid with an array of food in their cosy kitchen.

'You must be hungry, coming all that long way. Sit you both down and don't be shy. I'll make a pot of tea,' said Joan.

Sarah was so unused to being waited on that it all felt like a dream. She was hungry too. Joan pressed food upon them, brawn and pickles, fresh bread and butter, eggs, hard-boiled, and a vast choice of cakes and tarts. She could see that Joan was itching to ask questions, to know all about her; she was that kind of person. But very soon after the last cup of tea had been drunk, it was time to set off for the tent in the meadow.

People were already hurrying to the tent, dressed in their Sunday best. Joan was greeted on every side; evidently this was the kind of place where everyone knew everyone else. Inside the tent was a dimmer world enclosed by canvas, rows of chairs set out on grass. There was a subdued buzz of conversation as everyone took their seats.

'Thank goodness it's been dry lately,' whispered Joan to her cousin. 'Just think what it would be like if it was all mud underfoot!'

The hum of voices fell silent as a black-clad man entered the tent and strode to the lectern that had been placed in front, facing the audience. He was medium height, stocky, in his forties, Sarah guessed, bare-headed, with a head of thick, sandy-brown hair, and a Bible under his arm. He placed it on the lectern and faced the audience. Joan had confided over tea that this man had a younger brother, George, also a preacher, who had a reputation for being 'like a lion', his sermons fiery and passionate, striking the hearers with the fear of hell and judgement to come, having them trembling in their seats and praying for forgiveness. Sarah had half-expected his brother to be the same. But Stephen Jeffreys seemed different. His eyes were as blue as the summer skies, and as he looked over the assembled people, they seemed to hold a twinkle.

Sarah had been half-wishing she had not come since that teatime conversation. They heard enough of that kind of preaching at chapel week by week, and often at Fferm Fach too, filling her with guilt and a resolve to try harder to live up to God's standards. How on earth Beth could actually dare to be angry with God, she couldn't imagine.

She wondered again why her friend had wanted to come here so badly.

When Stephen Jeffreys began to preach, everything else was forgotten. Afterwards, she could not recall the words he had used, the Scripture texts he had quoted – scarcely anything. But she never forgot the story of his own conversion and how his life was changed after an encounter with the Saviour, Jesus Christ. Born in the Welsh valleys into a poor background, he had no option but to become a coal miner, and worked in the mines for eight years or more. He and his brother had both responded to the message of salvation through Jesus, as had so many others during the time of the 'Welsh Revival' soon after the turn of the century. Both had given up their jobs and devoted their lives to preaching that gospel message. In the telling of his story, the ex-miner sometimes related little anecdotes that brought a smile to the lips and even a subdued ripple of laughter. His blue eyes twinkled and made Sarah want to laugh too, but she stopped herself, slightly horrified. Laughing in a church service? Whatever would the Hughes family and the chapel people think about that? Church and chapel services were no place for frivolity, and one must be reverent and solemn. She stole a sideways look at Beth and saw that she was struggling for composure too, so did not dare look at her again in case they should disgrace themselves.

It was strange, but she didn't think that Stephen Jeffreys would have minded one bit if they'd laughed out loud. He looked out over his audience and told them that the love of Jesus reached out to each and every one of them. He spoke gently, did not strut or rant, but nevertheless everybody in the tent listened with rapt attention.

Everyone seemed thoughtful as they left the tent and made their way homeward. Even the talkative Joan was unusually silent. Sarah was suddenly very tired after the long day's travelling, and her muscles, unused to horseback riding, were beginning to stiffen. She could not have described how she was feeling – a mixture of curiosity, new ideas, a strange little flicker of excitement, and a desire to know more. The gospel message preached by Stephen Jeffreys was the same one she'd heard Sunday by Sunday, and yet it was different. She couldn't have described the difference, but it was there.

Joan made cocoa for them all and found her voice again. 'Well, that wasn't quite what I expected. I shall go again tomorrow night, though. What a pity you two couldn't stay another day.'

Beth sighed. 'I know, I was thinking the same. But I couldn't. Glyn will be expecting me home tomorrow and he would be so worried if I didn't come, and no way of sending to tell him. And Sarah has her work to go to.'

Sarah thought longingly of how wonderful it would be to stay longer. But of course she must get back. What on earth would Eira Hughes say if she did not return tomorrow? She sighed, and could not quite stifle a yawn.

'There, bach, you're tired out,' said kind Joan. 'It's been a long day for you. Your bed is all ready, made up and waiting.'

Later, tucked up in a feather bed in Joan's spare room, with clean cool sheets smelling of lavender, Beth mentioned the meeting again.

'After what Joan said, I was expecting a fiery kind of preaching, like she said the other Jefferys brother did. But this one wasn't a bit like that. No lion about him at all.'

Sarah agreed. Beth went on wistfully, 'That look in his eyes when he talked about Jesus, as though the love of Jesus was the most real thing in the world. As though all that about dying on the cross was not because God was angry, but because of love. He needn't have done it, he was the Son of God, but he did it for us. Humble and meek, like a lamb.'

A lamb. The lamb of God.[3] That exactly described the way Stephen Jefferys portrayed Jesus. Sarah's tiredness seemed to fall away. 'Oh, I wish I knew more!'

'So do I,' said Beth. She yawned suddenly. 'It's been such a long day. I think it's time we went to sleep.'

Sarah agreed. In spite of all the thoughts buzzing in her mind, her eyes would scarcely stay open. Beth blew out the candle and they were both asleep in seconds.

Next day, having been served a hearty breakfast by Joan, provided with food for the journey and made their goodbyes, with warm invitations to come again, they were leaving Michaelchurch Escley and setting the horses' heads towards home. They rode in silence for a while, thankful for another dry day, listening to the birdsong in the hedgerows and the soft snorting of the horses' breaths

---

3. See John's Gospel, 1:29,36.

and thump of their hooves. But the events of the previous evening were still fresh in their minds.

'I've been thinking,' said Beth after a while. 'We couldn't stop for more meetings but, you and I, if you came over on your half-days – we could pray together, couldn't we?'

This was a new idea to Sarah. Praying happened in chapel, didn't it? The preacher praying and the congregation respectfully bowing their heads. Did they all pray, Sarah wondered, or just listen, or did their minds wander? Hers often did. There were prayers at Fferm Fach too, led by Penry Hughes, with the children often sighing and fidgeting and sometimes earning a sharp reprimand. But, two women praying together in a farm kitchen? She felt a stirring inside, a longing to know more about the God Stephen Jefferys preached, the gentle, loving God who had given his Son as a sacrifice for the sins of the whole world. She felt the longing grow stronger.

'Yes,' she said. 'I'd like to do that.'

They rode again in silence. Sarah suddenly realised her friend seemed different today. She said with a new boldness, 'Beth, you don't seem to be angry with God any more.'

Beth looked across at her. Even her face seemed different, softer, with some of the little frown lines gone. She nodded and said, sounding almost as surprised herself, 'No, I'm not. I still don't understand about Evie – and a lot of other things. But I know now that God is real. And oh, I want to know more!'

Sixteen

In the coming days, things seemed much the same as usual at Fferm Fach. Just as busy, or even busier, with the spring bringing its usual quota of new young creatures with their various needs and the predicaments they might find themselves in. The dangers to young animals seemed to be myriad – foxes with cubs to feed were on the lookout for vulnerable young chicks, ducklings and goslings, or lambs that were weak or recently born. There were carrion crows always watching out for weak animals. In addition, there were always the lambs whose mothers had died, or rejected them, or hadn't sufficient milk for twins or even the occasional triplets. These had to be bottle fed, a difficult task to begin with, when weak or cold ones had to be brought into the kitchen to be revived and warmed and coaxed to feed. The bigger bottle-fed ones soon became bold and demanding, expecting to be fed every time a human appeared. While one gobbled greedily from the bottle, the others would butt and push, impatient for their turn. But Sarah had a soft spot for the creatures and liked the feeding times.

Indoors, the baby cut more teeth and let the whole household know it. He was beginning to crawl and get underfoot. A construction of chairs and rails was built in a corner of the kitchen to restrain him, which he resented bitterly. The old lady complained and demanded attention, the boys squabbled and fought, Nancy withdrew into herself and Alice declared her intention of leaving home as soon as she was old enough. Mr Hughes worked long hard days and read his Bible morning and evening, and his wife was constantly overworked and bone-tired, and took out her frustrations on Sarah as often as not.

But the bright spot in all of this was Sarah's half-day when she would escape across the fields to Y Dyffryn, where Beth would have arranged her own work so that she and Sarah could spend the afternoon together. At first, Sarah had felt awkward about praying with someone else; prayer was something that happened in chapel or when Mr Hughes led family prayers – quite long and drawn out in less busy times, but considerably shorter at others.

'Should we just pray quietly to ourselves?' she asked Beth nervously the first time, anxious to get it right.

Beth seemed not too sure, either. 'Why don't we try just talking to God and telling him what's on our minds?' she said.

Sarah didn't quite know what to think about that, and felt a moment of panic. What was the correct way to address God? She tried to remember how the preachers in chapel began their prayers. She couldn't even quite remember what Mr Hughes said when he prayed at home, except that he repeated a lot of Scripture verses and long-drawn-out quotes, which made her turn her mind to other things and got the children fidgeting and sighing. It was quite a relief at busy times when the family prayers were considerably shortened. The idea of praying aloud herself was completely new. What if she made a mistake? What if God was angry with her?

'Can we do that?' she asked uncertainly, in reply to Beth's remark.

'I think so,' said Beth. 'Before we went to Michaelchurch, I'd have laughed at the very thought. I was that angry and confused after I lost my Evie, I could hardly believe in God at all. But there was something about that man – I don't know, but I had the feeling that he was like Jesus somehow, and Jesus would know all about me and love me just the same.'

'Well, you start, then.'

Somehow, sitting there at Beth's table in her cosy kitchen, all the doubts fell away. Beth began to pray aloud, hesitantly at first, but gaining in confidence. She poured out her heart, sometimes with tears, talking of her grief and confusion, her doubts and fears and longings. Sarah felt tears trickling down her own cheeks too. And when Beth paused for a moment, she found herself praying also, using her own words and feeling that it was perfectly all right.

After a while, the two of them paused and looked at each other, smiling tremulously. 'Well,' said Beth. 'Well. I think we could do with a cup of tea, don't you?'

They dried their eyes and sipped tea. Sarah felt rather astonished at the happenings but also strangely lighter, and with a strong desire to pray more. But it would soon be time for Glyn to come in for his tea, and the evening work to do.

'How time has flown,' said Beth. 'Come again soon, won't you?'

'I will,' promised Sarah.

She did, on her very next half-day. But this time she was in tears almost as soon as she crossed the threshold.

'Sarah, bach, whatever is it?' Beth hurried across the room, her face full of concern. 'Has something happened? Are you in trouble with Eira Hughes?'

Sarah shook her head. 'No, nothing like that. It's – it's – yesterday I had a letter from my mother . . .' She sat down at the table and buried her face in her hands.

Beth sat down too, taking Sarah's cold hands in hers. 'Is she ill? Or one of the family?'

'No, no. Maybe I'm just being foolish. But nothing will ever be the same again. Here, you'd better read it for yourself.' She pulled a rather creased envelope from her apron pocket and thrust it at Beth, who read it with a little frown between her eyes.

Afterwards she handed the letter back to Sarah and said thoughtfully, 'I can see why you're upset. But maybe it's not all bad. Maybe some good will come from it.'

Sarah felt the tears spring to her eyes again. 'I don't see how! How can it? Things will never be the same again!' She fumbled for her handkerchief.

'There, there, don't start again or you'll set me off too,' said Beth. 'I'll make some tea and we'll talk about it.'

Sarah sipped her tea and talked, and found that it did help, and the knot of misery that had settled in her stomach seemed to ease a little. She even gave a shaky kind of laugh. 'Now you'll think I'm silly, soft in the head or something.'

Beth didn't laugh. She said, 'No, I can see how upset you are.' She paused for a moment. 'How would it be if we prayed about the whole thing? For everyone concerned, and for you to be comforted and have peace in your heart?'

Sarah gulped. 'I never thought of that.'

As they prayed, she had the same feeling that she'd had before, a kind of quieting and comforting, a sense that they were somehow on the way to finding something else. She didn't know exactly what. But she knew that Beth had the same feeling too. A longing for something more.

She had no idea what that might be. Until the morning that everything changed.

CHAPTER

Seventeen

Mrs Hughes had decided that they must make butter that morning. Another cow had recently calved, so there was a surplus of milk and cream. As soon as the children had departed for school, she collected her milking buckets and set off to the cowshed, leaving Sarah to prepare the dairy. The big churn had to be pulled out from its corner, thoroughly scrubbed inside and out, and scalded with a kettle of boiling water. Then the same with the wooden butter-worker – a long table where the solid curds would be rolled with wooden rollers, to squeeze out the last remaining moisture, salted, and slapped and moulded with the wooden paddles known as 'hands', formed into oblong blocks, weighed, stamped with a special marker and transferred to greaseproof paper on the cool stone slabs. The morning's milk would be separated from its cream by means of a galvanised metal machine with a large metal bowl on top and a system of tubes and pipes from which the cream would pour into a waiting crock, and the skimmed milk into a bucket to be consumed by the pig. The separating process involved a lot of twice-daily work; after use, the whole thing had to be dismantled and thoroughly washed in hot soapy water, every pipe and tube and tiny valve, and then put back together again. Everything in the dairy must be scrupulously clean. And butter-making took the whole day.

There were bright spots, though. Buttermilk from the churn was a delicious, slightly sour but refreshing drink, and they often made buttermilk pancakes in a big iron skillet over the fire. Most of the butter went to the market, but there was enough for the family too, and there was nothing more delicious than fresh butter on crusty bread.

Sarah rolled up her sleeves and prepared for a hard day. First, the churn had to be scrubbed and scalded. The crock of soured cream stood waiting on the long stone slab.

She had finished the churn and was waiting in the warm kitchen for the kettle to boil when she became aware that she was not alone in the room. She looked round but there was no one. She thought she heard old Mrs Hughes cry out, and that she should go to her, but suddenly her feet felt rooted to the spot. Then came a feeling that her knees were weak, her strength ebbing, and next moment there was a stronger sense of someone there, unseen but so real, someone who loved her more than she could ever know, who knew her name and everything about her. She gasped. This was the feeling she'd had in that tent, that seemed to be a part of Stephen Jefferys, but magnified a myriad times. 'Jesus,' she whispered. And she knew without doubt that it was he, not far away in heaven but there beside her in the stone-flagged kitchen. She couldn't tell how long she stood there, hands clasped, just basking in the love that seemed to flow over her in great waves. She never noticed that the kettle was coming to the boil and that the old lady had called out again. Nothing seemed to matter except that wonderful presence. 'Oh Jesus,' she whispered. 'You're real! And you love me! I'm so sorry for doubting you and all the other wrong things. I know you died for me. And I love you too. Please don't ever leave me!'

And the words came into her mind, words that she had heard many times from her chapel pew. She could even remember that it was in the book of Hebrews, chapter 13, verse 5: 'I will never leave thee, nor forsake thee.' She felt the tears wet on her cheeks.

The kettle boiled over and hissed into the flames. Sarah came to her senses and seized the kettle holder to place it on the hob. She called out to the old lady, 'I'm coming, Mrs Hughes!' And then she glanced out of the window and saw something that halted her in her tracks. Eira Hughes had stopped in the yard, obviously on her way back from milking. She had placed the two full buckets on the muddy ground and was on her knees between them, hands raised, eyes closed and a look of rapture on her face. At the same moment, old Mrs Hughes appeared at the door of the parlour, on her feet and walking without her stick. She said, 'Oh Sarah!' and clasped the girl in her thin arms. Sarah felt her own arms go round the old lady. She remembered, with a sense of wonder, that old Mrs Hughes had never addressed her by her name before – she'd always been just 'the girl'. Sarah felt suddenly overcome by remorse at the resentment she'd felt. She hugged the old lady tightly, and helped her to the armchair.

Eira had picked up the milk buckets. Sarah realised that her work had been left half-done and hurried to take the buckets through to the dairy. Overwhelmed by the feelings of love and remorse that swept over her, she went back to the kitchen, but before she could open her mouth to utter a word, Eira was saying, 'Oh Sarah, I'm so sorry for the way I've mistreated you so often, blaming you for things that weren't your fault, expected too much. I saw it all in a flash. Jesus came to me. I told him I'm sorry for all my sins and he forgave me. Will you forgive me too?'

Sarah struggled to understand all that she was hearing. 'What happened?'

At that moment the door opened and Penry Hughes came in. He had not long departed for his morning's work and was never indoors at this time. He had a dazed expression on his face and sat down heavily at the table. His wife and Sarah stared at him in wonder.

'I had a visitation,' he said. 'In the field, out topping mangels, and all of a sudden—' he paused, his hand over his eyes. 'It was the Lord! Wife, it was like scales dropped from my eyes and I could see what manner of man I've been. I've been a religious man all my life, but I never knew him. Not until now. I've tried to live a good life and please God, but I was doing it in my own strength. I had to cry out for mercy! And he saved me! He saved me!'

He seemed quite overcome. The women looked at each other in amazement. At the very same time, on the same day, the very same revelation had come to them all. Even the baby, usually grizzling and demanding attention, was sitting contentedly in his corner, playing with a wooden wagon.

Old Mrs Hughes spoke up, her voice not the usual complaining one, but strong and steady. 'The Lord has been gracious to us and has been pleased to meet with us all. We shall never be the same again, praise his name.'

She got to her feet and walked steadily across the room. 'I shall get dressed and cease to be a burden. Oh, hallelujah!'

The door of the parlour closed behind her.

'Well,' said Eira. 'Well. Whatever next? The Lord is good! But I suppose we must get on, the work won't do itself. But Mother is right. We shall never be the same again!'

Eighteen

Things never were the same again. Sarah could never have imagined the changes that came to them all at Fferm Fach, all seemingly in the blink of an eye. Eira Hughes had come to her again that same day with tears in her eyes, saying how sorry she was for the way she had taken out her frustrations on Sarah and often been unkind. Sarah had been tearful too, full of remorse for the resentments and bitterness she had so often felt. The two of them had embraced, there in the cool salty dairy, with a pile of butter curds waiting on the butter-worker and buckets of buttermilk around them.

Mr Hughes had gone back to his work with a new peaceful and gentle look replacing his usual sour and careworn expression, and even the baby was more content, laughing and gurgling whenever he was spoken to. Most remarkable of all was the transformation of the old lady, who seemed infused with new life. She was as good as her word, dressing without assistance, tying an apron on and announcing her intention of preparing the potatoes and carrots for dinner. The children, when they came home, seemed changed too, maybe because of the new atmosphere, or maybe the Lord had somehow touched them too. At any rate, Alice seemed less discontented, Nancy not so timid, and the small boys played together quietly instead of fighting.

Sarah could not wait to tell Beth about the wonderful thing that had happened. But in the event, she did not have to wait, because the very next morning Beth came knocking at the door, flushed and excited. She was bubbling over with something and was hardly inside before she exclaimed, 'Oh Eira, Sarah, Mrs Hughes! Something wonderful happened yesterday morning, you'll never believe it—'

Eira Hughes laughed. 'About half-past nine?'

'Yes,' said Beth. 'However did you guess?'

And then there was a babble of talk, as they all told of the wonderful happenings of the day before. Sarah found herself sitting down with them at the table drinking tea, at Eira's invitation, something that had never happened before. Mrs Hughes usually expected her to go on with her work on the occasions of neighbours visiting. But now she said, 'Oh, sit down for a minute, Sarah! You've got as much to tell as any of us.' And the tea grew cold as they marvelled at the wonder of it all.

'I was up to my elbows in pastry dough, making a batch of rhubarb tarts,' said Beth. 'Glyn does love them. And I just had to stop and get down on my knees and the Lord met with me in that moment.' She clasped her hands. 'And – and – I knew that my Evie is with him, that she's safe and happy, and that I'll see her again. When I could get up, I went to tell Glyn, and there he was, in the barn, with his arms up in the air and the glory of the Lord all over him.'

There was something else. When the postman came, at dinner time next day, he had news for them. All of the dwellings in their area, mostly farms but a cottage or two as well, had experienced the same visitation at exactly the same time on the same day. 'It's all them can talk about,' said the postman, quite bewildered. 'Like that there Welsh revival come down on us here, or summat!'

'Shall we tell them at the chapel on Sunday what's happened?' wondered Eira one evening after family prayers. 'What will they make of it, I wonder?'

Family prayers had taken on a new kind of direction over the last few days. Everyone felt it, from old Mrs Hughes, who now joined them every evening, to the small boys, who now sat quietly and listened instead of fidgeting and yawning. Sarah was aware of something new and joyful about these gatherings round the kitchen table, a lightness and gladness and a desire to praise God, so different from the solemn reading of the Scriptures, the long, drawn-out prayers and exhortations to do better and try harder. Now it seemed something to look forward to, like meeting with a friend and getting to know them better. *That was it*, thought Sarah in wonder, *we're meeting with Jesus.*

'We shall,' said Penry Hughes in reply to his wife's question. 'We cannot keep something like this to ourselves, can we?'

Sarah thought how wonderful it would be if the whole congregation were blessed with this new experience too.

But it did not happen in quite that way. On Sunday, she could see that many of their neighbours had been truly touched as they had; it showed on their faces. They had brought old Mrs Hughes with them for the first time in years, helping her onto the quietest of the ponies, and walking slowly beside her across the mountain. The old lady was a little stiff in the joints from years of immobility, but determined to attend. 'I have wasted far too much time,' she said. At the chapel, the women crowded round as she was helped to dismount, exclaiming at the miracle of her recovery.

'The Lord touched me,' was all the explanation she could give.

Penry Hughes had a quiet word with the preacher, asking if he could share something during the service. Permission was given; after all, he was a respected elder of the chapel. When the time came, Sarah held her breath. Her employer stood, cleared his throat, and said simply, 'You see before you this morning a new man. I have attended this chapel since my birth, been proud to be an elder here, and considered myself a good Christian man. But it wasn't until this week that, by the grace of God, I realised my sinful state, and also by his grace, repented of it and was truly born again by the Spirit of God.'

A muted hubbub of voices broke out around the chapel building as he sought to explain just what had happened. Another voice chimed in, Jim Parry from Tynwern, saying, 'Penry's right. It happened to me too, and my missus.' And immediately more people, men and women, were getting to their feet, joining in, telling of their own experiences. The well-planned service was in disarray.

The faces of some of the elders were like thunder. The preacher quickly brought the meeting to a close. Afterwards, he went to each of the elders and deacons and informed them of a special meeting to be held the following evening at his home.

It was a slightly subdued group that made their way home across the mountain. Sarah wondered what was to come.

But nothing could subdue for long the joy that flooded her heart. That night, before she fell asleep, she remembered the words that Penry had so bravely spoken in the chapel, that he had been born again by the Spirit of God. That summed up her own experience. She had not written in her diary for several days, not knowing how to put it into words. But that was it exactly – she felt newborn, as though her life was beginning all over again. She wanted to record it somehow. It was far too late to light the candle and write in the diary now. But there was moonlight outside, shining into the room when she sat up in bed and pulled back the curtain. She found her pencil and in the light of the moon, she wrote on the plaster wall a few words: Sarah Rees, B July 22nd 1908. BA April 19th 1922.

The joy remained even when Monday morning came and there was a large pile of laundry to toil over. It was a grey day, with drizzle falling, so the washing had to be dried indoors on the airing rack, which meant the depressing sight of the shirts and petticoats and underwear of the whole family dangling damply over their heads when the rack was raised on its pulleys.

Everyone waited with bated breath for the return of Penry from his meeting that evening. He hung up his damp hat and coat and didn't speak for a moment.

'Well,' he said, sitting down in his chair, and then repeated himself. 'Well.'

'Well what, Penry?' asked his wife, putting down a cup of tea at his elbow. 'Tell us what was said.'

Her husband took a slurp of his tea and put down the cup heavily. 'Well,' he said again. 'A great deal was said.

Some of it not the most pleasant. Tempers were lost. But the outcome is, we are put out of the chapel.'

Several pairs of eyes stared at him. 'Put out?'

'Aye, asked to leave. We are not welcome there any more. None of us from that morning.'

Nobody spoke for a moment. Then Eira said, 'But – but – what shall we do? We've always gone there. We're chapel people. Oh–' She looked as though she might cry.

Penry cleared his throat. 'Don't fret yourself, missus. Some of us were talking, after. We want to go on worshipping altogether. That's what the Lord would want. Remember that verse that we should not neglect the assembling of ourselves together?'[4]

'But how can we ...?'

'There'll be a way,' said Penry. 'To begin with, we can meet outside, out on the mountain, even. We can praise the Lord wherever we are. We'll not lose the blessing that's come to us. If the weather's bad, we can go in one of our barns. Or our houses, if there's room enough. One day, we may even have a building of our own. Who knows where the Lord may take us?'

---

4. Hebrews 10:25, KJV.

CHAPTER

Nineteen

Amy, present day

Amy woke with the sudden realisation that the holiday was almost over – two more days and they would be leaving Fferm Fach and heading back to their everyday lives – home, school, friends. She could not believe how the time had flown. And she also realised that she did not want to leave. Not just to be away from the painful memories that waited at home, but she also knew that she would miss this little house perched on the mountainside, the peace, the bracken and whinberry-covered slopes that led up to the Bluff, the cries of the red kites and the sheep, even the mist that sometimes rolled down from the high peaks. She'd miss Beth and David and Y Dyffryn. She'd miss Sarah.

Dad had a little summing-up session at breakfast. Everyone was in agreement that it had been a good holiday. Dad and Mum were both pleased with the amount of research and writing they'd been able to do, the wonderful bookshops in Hay, the pure air and the breathtaking scenery. Dad had a little frown, however, when it came to the amount, or lack of, revision the girls had done. 'I've barely seen either of you open a book at all,' he said. 'You were supposed to do some work, at least.'

'Oh, but Dad,' said Emily. 'I've learned so much. I've had such a lot of hands-on experience! I've delivered twelve lambs, including twins, and a couple of the births had complications—'

She would have launched into precise details of the deliveries, had not Amy given her a sharp dig in the ribs. 'Shut up, Ems!'

Mum was regarding Amy thoughtfully. 'I must say you look a lot better yourself, Amy. Colour in your cheeks and you're eating well. I don't know what Ceri at Y Dyffryn has been doing, but she's been good for you.'

'However—' began Dad, but was interrupted by the buzzing of Amy's phone. Amy guessed he'd been about to say they should at least stay in and revise today. She got up and went to the window, where the reception was better.

It was Ceri, sounding excited. 'Hey! I don't know if you and Emily are planning on coming over today, but I've found something that might interest you. Something about Sarah that explains a lot of things.'

Amy felt a strong twinge of excitement. She looked across at her family, who all seemed to be looking at her too.

'Er, well—' she began, but Emily, guessing who it was, said quickly, 'If that's Ceri, then tell them yes, we'd love to go over.'

Dad sighed with resignation and said, 'Well, if you fail your exams and don't get your grades, don't blame me!'

'We'd love to come,' said Amy into her phone. 'Can't wait!'

On the way across the fields, her heart raced with anticipation. Emily went at once to the lambing shed, where

David greeted her with relief. Three or four bottle-fed lambs, 'tiddlings', were butting and pushing at his legs while he fed one of them from a bottle. He handed the bottle to Emily. 'Here, you take over. I've got lots to do as well as feed this mob. There's a couple of broken pens to mend, for a start.'

Amy left them to it and headed for the house. Ceri greeted her eagerly. 'You'll never guess! I started going through the other lot of papers – not the one you looked at – and found a whole lot of letters and more. Come into the sitting room.'

'Did you find the other part of Sarah's diary?' asked Amy.

'No, but what I found is even better, I think. I got so interested I was up half the night! I've tried to arrange things in order. Look!' She had made neat piles of what seemed to be envelopes. They were addressed to Mr and Mrs Henry Parry at Fferm Fach. 'They were some of the family, the ones that moved in after the Hugheses left.'

'Where did the Hugheses go?' wondered Amy, picking up the topmost one.

'Maybe you'd better read this first,' said Ceri. She picked up a yellowed page of what appeared to be a clipping from an old newspaper. 'Read it.'

The clipping seemed to be from a local newspaper with a blurred 1920s date.

'Local family sets sail for foreign climes,' read the headline and underneath, continued:

Mr Penry Hughes, his wife, Eira, and their five children, together with Miss Sarah Rees, today set off bravely on the first part of their long journey, which will end in the Far Eastern land of China. They will travel under the care of the East India Shipping Company. We wish them well in their new venture.

Underneath was a rather blurred photo of a place Amy recognised at once as Fferm Fach, though looking much smaller and more primitive than the cottage it was today. In front stood a formal group – a stocky, bearded man, a slight, small woman holding a fair-haired toddler, two boys looking uncomfortable in Sunday suits and three young girls. Mr Hughes wore black and so did his wife; the others all had black armbands on their sleeves.

'Oh,' said Amy. 'No old lady. She must have died.'

Ceri looked at her rather strangely. 'Oh, you mean the black clothes and armbands. What made you think it was an old lady?'

'Well...' Amy was a little confused all of a sudden. 'I think I must have been dreaming again. I was sure there was an old lady.'

'Well, never mind,' said Ceri. 'You're probably right.'

'Which of the girls is Sarah?' wondered Amy, peering at the picture. All of the girls looked about the same height and were dressed much alike in dark jackets over mid-calf-length skirts. There was a list of names under the photo, left to right, but the print was so small and blurry that she could not make them out. She peered closer.

'There's a magnifying glass here somewhere,' said Ceri. She rummaged around in a sideboard drawer and produced it. 'See if that helps.'

It did help, quite a lot. Looking through it, Amy could just make out the names. She read them out. 'Mr Penry Hughes, Mrs Eira Hughes, William Hughes, Edward Hughes, Thomas

Hughes. The girls are Alice Hughes, Nancy Hughes, and yes, Miss Sarah Rees. That one's Sarah.'

She pointed to the girl on the right of the group, holding the glass close over the newspaper and peering through. The details were still unclear, but she could make out a sweet-looking face and dark hair pulled back and fastened behind her head. She was looking very serious; in fact, when she moved the glass along the line, Amy could see that not one of the group was smiling.

'They look so solemn,' she said. 'Even the little one.'

Ceri grinned. 'I believe people didn't smile for photographs in those days,' she said. 'Having your photo taken was a serious business!'

Amy focused on Sarah again. 'I wish I knew more about her.'

'Well,' said Ceri. 'When you come to the letters, I think you'll learn a whole lot more. Lots of info there.'

Amy picked up the top letter of the pile, which seemed very thin and light. But before she could do more, there was a scraping of boots in the back porch and they heard the kitchen door open and the sound of voices. Ceri looked at the clock.

'Elevenses time,' she said. 'We'll have to come back to these later.'

CHAPTER

Twenty

Amy couldn't wait for elevenses to be over. As soon as the door closed behind the workers, she scurried back to the sitting room. Anticipating a long session, Ceri had lit the fire and it was warm and cosy. Amy's heart thumped as she picked up the first envelope, on which she could not quite make out the address or date.

'I put them in order as much as I could,' said Ceri.

The first letter was very brief, looking as though it had been hastily written on flimsy paper. 'Dear Mrs Parry ...' Amy looked up enquiringly at Ceri. 'Would that be someone at Y Dyffryn? Wouldn't they have called each other by their first names?'

Ceri pulled out a chair and sat down. She laughed. 'They were very formal in those days – even neighbours and friends, if they were married women, called each other by their titles and not their Christian names. Read on.'

Amy read:

Just a line to let you know we've arrived safely. Journey pretty bad. All seasick except Sarah and myself. V different here. V hot. Will write more when I have time. Best regards to both and trust you are keeping well. Eira Hughes.

Amy replaced the short letter in its envelope, put it carefully to one side and picked up the next one. This was clearly addressed to Mrs Elizabeth Parry at Y Dyffryn, and she recognised the handwriting.

'I think this one's from Sarah,' she said.

'Well, go on, then, open it!' said Ceri with a laugh.

This was a longer letter, and, yes, when she took a peek at the last page, she saw that it was indeed signed with Sarah's name.

She read:

Dear Beth, there is such a lot to tell you, and I haven't had a moment to take the time until now. I had intended to describe every bit of the journey, but then every one of us except Eira and me were laid low with seasickness, even Penry, who has never had a day's illness in his life. We were kept busy, I can tell you! But we're here now, and oh, it will all be so worth it, because we know we are in the centre of God's will, where everything comes from his dear hand. Our arrival was very strange, so much bustle and clamour, there are flies and insects and it's hot already though not summer yet, and the people stare at us in great perplexity, no doubt wondering why we have come here. I must say I sometimes wonder myself! But I know I am going to love the Chinese people. I can't wait to get to the Mission Station where there is a language school as well as a hospital, and really settle down.

Amy stopped reading. 'A Mission Station? What does that mean? And are they in China? What on earth was going on?'

'They were missionaries,' said Ceri. 'Britain sent out many missionaries in those days, although I should imagine it was rather unusual for a large family to go. Mostly it would have been couples, or single people – there were a large number of single women in those days following the huge losses of young men in the First World War. The missionaries were very brave. The earliest they'd be able to come home to visit their families would be five years. And many were sick or died from tropical diseases because of shortage of the right medicines, especially the children. It was a hard life with many sacrifices.'

Amy had only hazy ideas of missionaries. She had vague pictures in her mind of people in pith helmets and women in long dresses.

'Is that the end of the letter?' asked Ceri.

'Almost,' said Amy. 'She goes on:

I think everyone was surprised by the size of our family. And there's such a lot of luggage! It will all have to be loaded onto a mule wagon to take us to the Station. Imagine that! So I had better make this letter shorter than I intended as there will be a lot of packing to be done. I promise I will write more next time. Your loving friend, Sarah.

Amy could hardly wait to open the next letter. It began:

Dear Beth, well, we are settling in, after a fashion. Life here is so different to back home in Wales, like another world. The children have started lessons at the Mission School, and all of us are having language studies every morning. I am doing well with mine. I hardly like to boast, but Alice and Nancy find it a lot harder and I have to help them a lot. It's possible they may go away to school in a year or two, the boys too when they are older, but they are studying here for the time being. I have been offered the chance to go away to study too, but oh, I love the work here so much, I am getting to know everyone and I get along with them. I really feel God wants me here, maybe to teach in the school myself later on. Eira goes to help at the hospital in the afternoons, the Chinese ladies come here to have their babies and they consider Eira something of an expert, having had so many herself! Penry can't wait to start helping with the Bible studies for men. Billy has a Chinese nurse, an amah, who looks after him, no easy task now he's toddling and very inquisitive. The Chinese just love Billy, they call him Didi, which means Little Brother, and can't get over his blond hair. They are always touching it to see if it's real, and squeezing his plump cheeks. The Chinese babies are very sweet, shiny dark hair, almond-shaped eyes and very solemn – or perhaps they're just puzzled when they look at us.

The letter went on to describe, in detail, life at the Mission Station, the daily routines, the characteristics of the people Sarah was getting to know, and it ended with:

I work hard but I am used to that! I am enjoying it all so much (or almost everything, the heat can be overwhelming and the insects! We even have to make sure the legs of our beds are standing in cups of paraffin so the lice can't crawl up, and some of the smells are pretty bad!). But that's a small price to pay. I am so happy! Your loving friend, Sarah.

The next letter had a slightly different tone; reading between the lines, Amy guessed that Sarah had been feeling a little homesick when she wrote it.

My dear friend Beth, it will be spring again in Wales now, and I do miss it, the green, the new lambs and chicks and goslings, the mountains, those lovely spring evenings with a blackbird singing. There is spring here too, of course, with the wheat fields greening over, and little bits of green and even flowers popping up wherever there is some soil to nourish them, but it is nothing like the green at home, even out on the mountain, and especially the hedgerows where it's just green upon green upon green. Do you remember that beautiful hawthorn with its creamy flowers we saw on the way to Michaelchurch Escley?

But please don't think I regret coming, I don't, not even for a minute. Ever since that other spring morning, I know that God has a plan for my life. And when I think of that letter and then the conversations I had with Mother, I realised he'd planned that I'd be free to go. As you know, I was a little upset when she told me she was marrying again, to Mr Thomas Powell, our neighbour and landlord, who we'd known all our lives, a good, kind man who would care for Walter and Graham as well and be a father to them. I knew things would never be the same again, she'd be moving into his farmhouse and our little cottage wouldn't be home any more. They both said I must consider the farm to be my home and I would be welcome there any time, and I knew they meant it, and that she and the boys would always be well provided for. But I was sad for a while, remembering how we'd been. And then – glory! – that morning came and everything was new! And the Hughes family are like my own now, and we love each other so much! Even the girls see me as a big sister, and that's what the Chinese call me, Jie Jie, which means Eldest Sister. That day changed everything, when Jesus truly came into all our lives and we were reborn! I wanted everyone to know, and share in the good news. I even wrote on my bedroom wall at Fferm Fach, just after it happened, just so that whoever came after might see it and know I'd been Born Again.

Amy put down the letter and looked at Ceri. 'So that's what it meant! The date that she was born and then the date she was born again, as she puts it!'

Ceri smiled. 'Yes, I'd sussed that out! She wanted everyone to know.'

The rest of the letter was in the same strain, gently reminiscing about her past life, but full of joy in the present and hope for the future.

Ceri got up and went to the kitchen to get on with her work. The clock ticked and the fire crackled. Amy read letter after letter, absorbed by the story as it unfolded. Some of the letters were short notes from Eira to the new occupants of Fferm Fach. Amy tried to work out their relationship to David and Ceri, but her head began to whirl and she decided she'd have to ask Ceri. Besides, it was much more entertaining to read the letters from Sarah to Beth, long and full of news and detail. She had a real gift for communicating, thought Amy. One of the letters read:

Beth, I was so excited to hear about the safe arrival of your little boy, Henry Joseph. I am so happy for you after what has gone before. God is good. Here, there is always great excitement at the birth of a boy, people dye hard-boiled eggs red and give them to their friends to celebrate, and they'd be setting off firecrackers and all kinds of things.

She sounds as though she's really enjoying the Chinese customs, thought Amy.

And as she read on, Sarah's letters were increasingly full of the work of the Mission, the struggles with language and customs and sometimes a funny story about a mistake that had been made. The church and school and hospital were expanding, and in spite of difficulties and setbacks, there were small encouragements and many rich experiences along the way. The work was not without its dangers; the missionaries were often required to travel to outlying villages, sometimes on bicycles. The roads were hazardous and bandits roamed the countryside. Illnesses waited to pounce upon the vulnerable and weak. Children were particularly susceptible, but so far the Hughes children had remained robustly healthy.

When Ceri came back into the room, Amy remembered the letter that had mentioned the birth of Beth's son, and fished it out of the pile. 'Would he be a part of David's family?'

Ceri thought for a moment, counting on her fingers. 'Yes, that little baby would be David's great-grandfather – I think. Goodness, those letters are a real slice of history, aren't they?'

Amy agreed. There were still things that puzzled her, though. 'Was that something that happened then, being born again?' she asked. 'I mean, why did it happen to only a few people?'

Ceri sat down, wiping her hands on her apron. She said, 'Well, I'm no expert on theology. I don't know why that day happened as it did. Only God knows that. But I know this, Jesus said that everyone could be born again;[5] in fact, it's the only way we can be made right with God. And what Jesus said then is the same today. Anyone can be born again, be forgiven for sins, have a fresh start in life.'

Amy stared at her. 'Really?'

Ceri smiled. 'Yes, really. I've been born again and so has David . . . It's for anyone and everyone.'

Amy found that her hands were trembling. She put down the letter. Something was melting inside her, something that had been kept tightly under control for a long time. And then she burst into tears.

---

5. See John 3:1-23.

CHAPTER
Twenty-one

Ceri leaned across the table and took Amy's hands. 'Amy, Amy, what is it? What's upsetting you?'

Amy's sobs quietened a little. She took out a tissue from a box on the table, and dabbed at her eyes.

'I – I don't know. It's just—' she choked back another sob that threatened to rise.

Ceri squeezed her hand and said gently, 'It might help to talk about what's bothering you. I know there's something. You look so sad sometimes, as though you're carrying the weight of the world on your shoulders.'

That's exactly it, thought Amy – there was a huge weight that she carried around with her wherever she went.

'It's just—' she began again, and then to her horror, heard herself say, 'I killed my best friend!'

There, she'd said it. She sobbed again. Now Ceri wouldn't want to be friends with her any more. Nobody would, if they knew.

Ceri might have been shocked but she didn't show it. She got up and pulled her chair round to Amy's side of the table. She sat down and put her arms round Amy and held her close. 'Do you want to tell me about it?'

Suddenly it was all pouring out, as though floodgates had opened and couldn't be closed. Amy gulped, took a breath, and said, 'Suzy and I had been friends for ages. From nursery, even, then primary school, and then high school. We both had other friends as well, but Suzy and me – we were special.' She paused. Ceri pushed the box of tissues nearer, and Amy mopped her eyes again. 'Suzy was a bit plump when we were little, but then she slimmed down and was really stunning. We did each other's hair and make-up and swapped clothes and all that. Someone said we ought to try modelling, and Suzy really liked the idea; well, we both did. We even did a couple of shoots for a local magazine. But then, Suzy started to think she was too fat. She wasn't, she was absolutely gorgeous and as slim as anything. But she thought we should both go on a diet, so we did for a while. It was awful. I was hungry all the time and then I fainted at school. My parents found out, they put their foot down and made me eat properly. But Suzy was sneaky about it. She kept on secretly dieting and got thinner and thinner.' She gulped again. 'She ended up in hospital after her parents took her to the doctor, and they said she was anorexic.'

Ceri nodded.

'She had some kind of hospital treatment, she didn't talk much about it,' Amy went on. 'We'd always told each other everything but she got very secretive. Anyway, she came home and said she was eating properly again. I wasn't sure about that. She always wore baggy tops and always trousers, never shorts or miniskirts or even leggings, so you couldn't see how thin her legs were. She got out of gym at school with some excuse that she made up about the hospital diagnosis – she never told me what it was, but I guessed it wasn't real. And then one day I had a glimpse of her ankles and they were so thin, like sticks, like they could snap at any moment.' The tears were running down her cheeks again now, as she remembered. Ceri waited. 'That day, Suzy and I had a bit of a row. She said she wanted some privacy and not to go barging into her room. But – but – I couldn't bear it. She was my best friend and after a couple of days I went round again. Her mum was so pleased to see me, she knew we'd fallen out and thought we'd made up. She said Suzy was in her room and pulled a face and said, "She hardly pokes her nose out at all, now it's the holidays. She's eating, though, quite well, although she insists on taking her food to her room. I make sure she shows me the plate afterwards, mind. Go on up, love."

'I went up, and didn't even knock, because I thought she'd tell me to go away. I opened the door, and – and—' Amy could not go on for a moment. 'And – she had her dinner plate in her hand, and her wardrobe door was open and there was this big plastic bag inside, and she was scraping the food into the bag. I only had a quick glimpse but I could see the bag was half full of food, and I could smell it was starting to go off a bit.' Amy felt sick, remembering. 'She didn't realise I'd seen. She just sort of whirled round, closed the wardrobe door and said, "Oh, Ames, I was just having my dinner." And she actually forked up a bit of cottage pie from her plate and ate it. I didn't know what to do. I was just so glad she was talking to me again. I went and sat on the bed like I always did. Suzy put her plate down on the bedside table and said, "Mum always gives me too much . . .

I had a big lunch and I'm full." She patted her stomach and I saw how dreadfully thin she was under the big T-shirt.

'I didn't say a word about what I'd seen, I was just so pleased to be friends again, and we lay on the bed and listened to music like always. I guessed she'd been scraping food into that bag for ages, sneaking out to the bin with it when the coast was clear. I knew I should tell her mum and dad but I didn't.'

Amy was shaking with sobs now. Ceri got up and fetched a glass of water from the kitchen. 'You needn't say any more if it's all too much,' she said gently.

Amy took a drink and felt better. She said, 'No, I want to. I've wanted to tell someone for ages. I knew I should say something about what she'd been doing, but I didn't. I had this idea I'd be betraying her, so I never said a word. And then – and then – it was less than a week later that they told me she'd died, in her sleep, of a heart attack. And it was all my fault.'

'No,' said Ceri 'That's not true—'

'But it is!' Amy interrupted her. 'Don't you see? If I'd said what she was doing, someone would have done something, put her back in hospital or something – I could have saved her and I didn't. It was my fault. I killed her!' She hid her face in her hands.

Ceri gently took them away. 'Look at me, Amy. You didn't kill your friend. No, listen to me. You could have spoken up, but I doubt that in the long run it would have made a scrap of difference. I've been a counsellor, remember? And I know that if someone in this situation makes up their mind on a course of action, it's very difficult to change it. People get crafty, they become very good at hiding things; sadly, all too often there are tragedies like this, but they happen.'

Amy's sobs had quietened. She said, in a small voice, 'But it shouldn't have happened to Suzy. I shouldn't have let it. I'll never forgive myself.'

There was quiet in the room for a moment, except for the ticking of the clock on the mantelpiece and the crackling of the fire. Then Ceri said thoughtfully, 'I understand that feeling. But – you don't have to do it all by yourself, you know. You remember what we were talking about before?'

Amy raised a flushed and tear-stained face and thought what a mess she must look. She said, 'You mean about having a fresh start?'

'Yes. If you ask Jesus to forgive you for that, and for everything else wrong you've ever done. You can start over again.'

'I – I don't know how,' said Amy wistfully. 'Should I go to church?'

Ceri smiled and patted her knee. 'Well, that would be good. But you just need to ask, to pray, here and now, and God will hear.'

'Can you help me? Should I kneel down?'

'No need. That wooden floor's a bit rough anyway and you might get splinters in your knees! I'll pray first, then you just say whatever you want.'

Amy's thoughts were whirling. She hardly heard Ceri's prayer, except that it seemed like someone talking to someone else here in the room with them. She had no idea what to say herself. But when she opened her mouth, she found herself saying simply, 'Jesus, I'm so sorry I didn't help Suzy. I'm sorry for everything wrong I ever did. Please help me and come into my life.' And then she added, because it seemed the right thing to do: 'Amen.' She asked Ceri, 'Is that it?'

'That's it, for a start. You'll learn more as you go along. But just believe that Jesus is in your life now and he'll never leave you. You're a new person. You're born again.' A strong smell of burning wafted in from the kitchen. Ceri shrieked, 'Oh! I forgot the potatoes. They'll have boiled dry!' She dashed into the kitchen, but was back in an instant.

'I'm so sorry,' said Amy.

'Oh, don't worry. I have some microwave chips that will do instead. And it's more than worth it. You can't compare a few burnt potatoes to someone really meeting Jesus. How are you feeling now?'

Amy had to think for a moment, but it took no longer than that to realise that the heavy load she'd carried for so long had lifted and gone. 'Different,' she said.

Two days later, the whole family stood outside the cottage at Fferm Fach for the last time. The car was waiting, packed with their luggage. The house door was locked, the key in Dad's pocket ready to return to David and Ceri when they called by on their way to say their final goodbyes. Unlike the day of their arrival, it was a mild, balmy day, the hillside behind the house bathed in sunshine, the sky blue with a few lazily drifting white clouds.

'I hate to go,' mourned Emily. 'There's so much going on here, and I'd love to see how those new triplets get on – we'll come back, won't we? Soon?'

'Yes,' said Mum. 'I think we all agree on that. It's been a terrific couple of weeks.' She exchanged a glance with Dad. 'I knew we'd love it, but we weren't quite sure about you girls—'

Emily sighed. 'It's been wonderful.'

'One last picture,' said Dad. 'Let's all stand in front of the house and get a selfie.'

'To add to the other sixty million,' said Emily. They posed and put on their best cheesy smiles.

'You're quiet, Amy,' said Mum as they walked towards the car. 'You've had a good time too, though, haven't you?'

Amy thought for a few seconds and then said simply, 'The best.'

She could not put into words her feelings. So far, she hadn't talked about her last morning at Y Dyffryn. She knew that a miracle had happened in her life, a miracle of discovery and forgiveness and a new peace replacing turmoil. A new beginning. One day soon, she would sit down with her family and tell them everything that had happened that day at Y Dyffryn, and the new quiet, hope and joy that she had. She wanted so much to tell them everything — to tell the world.

That morning, as she left her bedroom — Sarah's room — she'd looked again at the message on the wall. 'Thank you, Sarah,' she'd whispered. And then she'd fished a pen out of her bag and written her own inscription underneath Sarah's.

Just her name and the date she'd been born, followed by the date of the morning in spring when she'd been born again.

Author's Note

This story is fiction, and all the characters are fictional, the only exceptions being Stephen Jeffreys and the self-styled King of Hay, Richard Booth – who are real. Fferm Fach and Y Dyffryn are fictional farm names, but the setting and all other places mentioned are real. The story of the 'visitation' is based on a real happening in the early 1920s, which I have discussed with several of the descendants of the people involved, mostly farming families in a small area of the Black Mountains. Many of the descendants are now pastors, evangelists and church-planters in various places. My husband has a number of relatives who were impacted and whose ministries continue. I have included an abridged account of the 'Visitation' passed on to me by someone whose family was also involved. We do not know the exact date or day of the visitation, but for the purposes of the book have imagined it to be midweek.

Stephen Jeffreys

Stephen Jeffreys was born in South Wales in 1876 and worked as a coal miner for twenty-four years. In 1904, he was converted during the Welsh Revival, along with his younger brother, George. Both became evangelists, and travelled extensively to the United States, Canada, New Zealand and Australia as well as the length and breadth of the British Isles. Stephen was instrumental in setting up the Assemblies of God Church, pastored a church himself and preached to many hundreds of people, seeing many among them converted and becoming followers of Jesus.

The Visitation

Rising high, south from Hay-on-Wye, the peak of Hay Bluff dominates the end of a long ridge that borders England and Wales; to the west of the ridge stands the Twmpa. In between these two high places, a road runs through a gap that has been known for almost two millennia as the Gospel Pass. In the shadow of the Twmpa, half a dozen or more farmsteads spread westward across the landscape. The top hillside fields of Blaendigeddi Farm drop down from this narrow highway. It was here that William and Emily Greenow worked the land. The people who lived and worked in these places had one thing in common; one morning God came down to lighten the spiritual darkness of this enclave in the Black Mountains, and the light still shines today.

This was an extraordinary 'Visitation from Heaven'. The grown-ups were parents and neighbours of young married couples, and together with their servant workers, they were converted in an instant, at once, not little by little throughout the day.

Mrs Greenow and her husband were the only ones who attended the meetings of evangelist Stephen Jeffreys; the event that followed increasingly magnified God in his sovereign grace.

Until now I have always referred to this Visitation as 'revival', but I can no longer say this, because this working was a 'new beginning'. Nothing was there on the ground other than a dead religion, and immediately the testimony of these new gospel people brought opposition. They (the local community) had been religious. They attended regularly a small Baptist chapel – Penyrheol. I can remember walking across to this meeting place in the centre of a good-sized field.

Six months or so before the dawn of this new day, a lady who had moved from London to live near Michaelchurch Escley arranged for a large tent to be pitched alongside the road in a field, and invited Stephen Jeffreys to come to conduct a series of meetings. He came and went. There was no one who answered any call of the gospel. Mrs Greenow never talked about any healing of the sick taking place. In short, she was quite emphatic in saying, 'Nothing happened.'

Yet she also felt constrained to attend all the meetings. In order to be there, she and her husband made the journey on horseback. It was almost a twenty-mile round trip by road, around Hay Bluff. It was gosling-hatching time. When goslings come out of the shell, they need to be lifted out of the liquid aftermath so that they do not wallow in the deep shells. They cannot climb out. The likelihood of drowning is very high. The Greenows prayed, left the eggs and went to the meetings. They never lost a single hatchling. They were delivered by the hand of God. This was a great test and testimony. Loss at this season would mean that the years-end income would be substantially low. Not only would there be no geese at Christmastime, but no 'followers' to replenish the laying stock and in time not enough eggs either to sell or to retain for hatching. While they were still unbelievers they saw the goodness of God.

That morning, Mrs Greenow's brother, Will Price, was out at work 'butting and topping' swedes (pulling them out of the ground and cutting off the leaves and roots). That is where he was converted. Mrs Greenow was carrying milk to the dairy. After putting the pails down in the middle of the yard, she came to the Lord on her knees. On another farm, her sister, Ada, had a very powerful encounter with the Lord. Around this time, Ada passed away, leaving a husband and one-month-old baby, David. When she died, there was a mighty 'rush' of the Holy Spirit into her bedroom. Her hair was swept into the air and brought down perfectly into place as though it had been brushed and combed. By a gentle work of the 'hand of God' her hair was set perfectly, a testimony to remember that 'precious in the sight of the LORD is the death of his saints'.[6] Emily Greenow took her sister's baby and looked after him for a while until he could return to his father's care. Later he became a much-beloved evangelist who settled in Northern Ireland but travelled the world preaching the gospel. Sadly (but with a blessed outcome) all those who had experienced this 'new beginning' were ejected from Penyrheol chapel. The first meeting of the new company was held immediately, worshipping the Lord in the open air in a field. Afterwards they met in some hall or other in Hay on Sundays, and on week nights met at the Greenow Farm. When the news of the ejection reached him, a speaker called David James came up through the pass to meet with them midweek

---

6. Psalm 116:15, KJV.

until there was no further need. Eventually a Gospel Hall in Lion Street, Hay, was built on land purchased by a group of the farming people for the sum of £50, and later still came the purchase of a red-brick Primitive Methodist chapel in Oxford Road, Hay, 'Bethesda' where the gospel is preached to this day.

Many of the children and grandchildren of the original families have gone on to become preachers, evangelists, church-planters and pastors, the legacy of the 'Visitation' continuing.[7]

---

7. Extensive enquiries have been made to trace the author of the above account, but we have been unable to identify them. Edited for the purposes of this book.

Further Reading

Marcus Thomas, *David Greenow: His Life & Legacy* (Maurice Wylie Media, 2020).

Edward Jeffreys, *Stephen Jeffreys: The Beloved Evangelist* (Tamworth: Elim Publishing Company, 1946).

Further Resources

ISBN: 9781910786659

Lizzie couldn't believe it. She had just gone to the hospital for a quick check-up and now they told her she could die. The doctors had diagnosed Anorexia and that she must regain weight. Her life closed in around her, but all she wanted was to avoid food.

Anyone who lives with an eating disorder fights their own thoughts, their own anxieties, their own self, every second of every minute of every day. For Lizzie, this was her reality from the age of 14. However, through professional help, the support of her loving family and her faith, she somehow found the hope and strength to overcome. *Life Hurts* tells Lizzie's story, reflecting on it from her perspective as a doctor. Her vision is to inspire and encourage others to see that, although eating disorders can be devastating, there is hope for all of us.